Advanced Praise

"Swanson's vivid characters jumped off the page, grabbed me, and threw me into their ever-changing worlds. Each word drew me deeper into Fern's puzzle until I was so deeply engrossed in her story I forgot what was going on around me. I look forward to more from this talented, young author."

—**J. Anderson**, author of *The Breeding Tree*

"Swanson fuses winsome characters with wild imagination in this shining debut."

—**Rosalie Valentine**, reviewer & blogger

"*The Girl Who Could See* stole my breath away. It is a story of fierce hope, yearning, and intensity that captured my soul from start to finish and lingered in my heart like a friend."

—**Bethany A. Jennings**, author of *Threadbare*
& *Dragon Lyric*

"Kara Swanson weaves a gripping tale with unique characters and a dynamic world that will grab your attention from the very first page and keep you reading until all hours of the night!"

—**Mandy Fender**, author of the *Defier* series

"The Girl Who Could See beautifully blends the genres of fantasy and sci-fi together into a suspenseful read that kept me on the edge of my seat! The deep journeys these characters experience in a short novella is amazing. Perfect for a summer read at the beach. "

—**Rachelle Rea Cobb**, author of the
Steadfast Love series and *Write Well*

"The Girl Who Could See is a MUST read. Kara Swanson is a masterful storyteller with a flair for the extra-ordinary. Swanson catapults you into the story, taking hold of every sense you have and refusing to let go until you've read the very last word."

—**JC Morrows**, author of the best-selling
Order of the MoonStone series

"Written in an excellent first person point of view that makes for an intriguing plot that moves you alongside Fern, the girl who could see. Fans of Lisa T. Bergren and Sara Ella should love this novella. From the very first page, I was pulled into Fern's world(s), and didn't want to put it down!"

—**Lindsey Zimpel**, *Books for Christian Girls*

"Kara Swanson's novella pulses with action and beats with a love that longs to look beyond self. It's a vivid, imaginative story that encourages you to see what the world refuses to accept. An exciting read!"

—**Amber Stokes**, author of *How a Star Falls*

"I'll be the first to say that Kara Swanson's book, *The Girl Who Could See*, is not a typical genre for me. But I promised I would stretch my reading self this year and branch out. I don't think I could have picked a better choice to stretch out with. This book is not just well-written, but creative, fast-paced, well-developed (especially for a novella!), and just…something I love. I was glued from the first sentence. And am so happy I branched out. So. Incredibly. Worth. It."

—**Mikal Dawn**, author of *Count Me In*

"For fans of Veronica Roth, Mary Weber and Sara Ella, Kara Swanson's *The Girl Who Could See* is a young adult wonder. Brimming with expert characterization, snap-crackle-and-pop dialogue and building a colorful world resplendent with magnetic and surprising descriptions, Swanson packs a punch—and an entire universe—into a novella that begs to be read in one sitting."

—**Rachel McMillan**, author of the
Herringford and Watts series

"At the intersection between two worlds comes a uniquely imaginative tale of love, epic triumph, and the power of one girl's mind."

—**Barbara Hartzler**, author of *The Nexis Secret*

THE GIRL WHO COULD SEE

THE
Girl
WHO
COULD
See

KARA SWANSON

Book Cover Design: Seedlings Design Studio

ISBN-13: 978-1542515481

ISBN-10: 1542515483

Dedication

To the countless people in my life who have believed the impossible—even when the rest of the world said you were crazy. You are my heroes. My inspiration. And to the Impossible—You are my hope.

Dear Reader,

Story inspiration usually comes to me in little trickles of whimsy—an image or song that sparks an idea. For the novella you hold in your hands, it came in two short sentences. Sentences that had me desperate to discover what story lay there. I hope you enjoy the journey as much as I did!

They say every child had an imaginary friend.

Mine never left.

Chapter One

Present Time

On television crime shows, they never tell you how cold it is.

They might show the dimly lit room with the hard, uninviting chairs. Or the narrow table separating you from the elderly agent with stone-gray eyes. But a TV camera cannot fully portray the chilling experience of an FBI interrogation.

I rub my bare shoulders, fingertips even icier than the skin exposed by my red tank top. *Brilliant move, Fern. Wearing a scarf but forgetting your jacket.* Stifling a shudder, I meet the sharp gaze of Agent Barstow, who stands at attention across from me.

"I don't know where you're from, Miss Johnson, but in LA, state-of-the-art buildings don't just crumble." His voice is gravelly, matching the jagged lines of his dark skin and weathered face. "Especially federal buildings."

I tug on my beige scarf. *You have no idea.*

His arms slowly unwind from his chest as he takes two steps toward me. "We've called in everyone to analyze this disaster. CIA, local police, firemen. Heck…we even called NASA. No one can come up with a plausible reason why a skyscraper in excellent condition would be standing one minute and collapse the next."

I fight the urge to bolt for the door as he leans down, palms flat on the table—so close I can make out the creases on his black suit.

"You warned us of an attack in that area over a week ago. How did you know?"

I suck in a deep breath as his voice lowers and his fists tighten on the edge of the table.

"Are you involved with a terrorist organization?"

I almost laugh at his words, which couldn't be further from the truth. I'm here to save LA, not destroy it. To save everyone in it. And I don't have much time—none of us does. If I can't gain this man's trust, a shattered building will pale in comparison to what comes next.

"No, sir." I shove my shaking hands beneath my legs.

A pair of lucid blue eyes appears over the agent's shoulder. I know not to stare. But those eyes, which only I can see, are the reason I warned the FBI in the first place. Their owner is the reason I'm sitting in this room.

Licking my lips, I keep my attention on Barstow. For years I've wanted someone to listen. Really listen. I didn't think the first person to do so would be in the FBI. *Be careful here.*

I open my mouth and force my voice to remain calm and steady. I hope my words are convincing— they *have* to be. "I knew about the incident, Agent Barstow, because my friend warned me." Throat dry, I look away. "My *imaginary* friend."

Chapter Two

Ten Days Earlier

Rubbing the creased fabric between my fingertips, I straightened the skirt of my mint-green waitress uniform. I snuck another glance at my watch as I hovered near the noisy kitchen door. It was that awkward time between meals, and business wasn't likely to pick up much in the next hour before my shift ended. Thank goodness. I had enough trouble concentrating without the bustle of the diner at closing time.

"Fern!" By the sharp tone of the cook's voice, I knew this wasn't his first attempt to get my attention. "Two burgers for table twelve. Before they're cold, if you don't mind."

I scooped up the platter, carefully balancing its lopsided contents. The cool plastic felt reassuring against my fingertips. Rigid. Real.

With careful steps, I navigated my way around tables topped in frilly red tablecloths and toward the waiting customers. As my dress swished about my knees, a teasing laugh tickled the edge of my ear, and I caught a few words before I could tune them out.

<What I wouldn't give for a decent meal, Plant Girl.>

My feet stopped abruptly. I hated it when he called me that. He'd been using the ridiculous nickname—a play on my name, Fern—since I was young.

Shaking my head to erase the lingering voice that echoed in my head, I mentally scolded myself for even admitting I'd heard him. For years, a revolving door of psychiatrists had encouraged me to ignore him. Ever since my imaginary friend entered my life when I was eight, on the heels of a trauma none could give me answers to.

Forcing one foot in front of the other, I crossed the diner, resisting the urge to peek over my shoulder. If I let myself look, I knew I'd see tousled blond hair. Dancing blue eyes. Blood and dirt caked on the side of his jaw.

Tristan. A young man who didn't exist.

"Hey, is that our order?"

The words jerked me back to the moment, and I turned my focus to the couple at table twelve. The woman leaned forward, her ample weight bulging against her thin dress as she waved in my direction. I maneuvered through the cluster of tables, balancing the precarious milkshakes, burgers, and fries.

When I was about three feet away, a rusted metal beam burst through the floor in front of me, jutting through the black-and-white checkered tiles with a grinding screech. I lurched away with a scream. My knees buckled.

A strong hand cupped my elbow and another held my waist, steadying me. But the tray continued its forward momentum, sending two Big Belly Burgers, two strawberry shakes, and an army of fries flying through the air—all over the shocked customers.

For a horrifying moment, the entire restaurant went silent. Then the tubby woman, now covered in pink slime, let loose a mangled shriek.

"I'm so sorry..." I began. But when I turned back, the twisting sheath of metal was gone. Not even a crack marred the checkered ground beneath my red tennis shoes.

Instead I found *him*. With that infernal smirk and almost-translucent muscled frame towering over me. He had caught me—just like he'd been doing since I was a child. Not that anyone else would believe it.

Breathe. In. Out.

I'd had another hallucination.

"It's ruined!" It took me a moment to realize the woman was addressing me. "What do you plan to do about this?" She gestured to the food coating her dress.

Get fired, probably. The thought made my chest clench. I needed the income to take care of my niece. I'd lost two other jobs in the past six months. I couldn't afford to lose this one.

"I-I'm sorry." My voice shook as much as my hands.

My manager stormed toward us. While the lady ranted about how expensive her dress was and he tried to calm her with soothing words and promises of full refunds, I used up three silver canisters of paper napkins to wipe up the shake and hamburger remnants clinging to the table and floor. I'd learned quickly after returning home all those years ago that that was the best way to survive—quietly. Not drawing attention. Not speaking up.

But, somehow, proving my shrink and family wrong, nonetheless. Proving that I could function just like anyone else. That I was strong enough to take care of myself and those I cared about.

After the couple stormed out, my manager turned to me. He let out a bedraggled sigh. "Fern—"

"It won't happen again. Please, just give me one more chance."

He rubbed a hand over his mouth. "You're one of the hardest-working waitresses on staff, so I'll let it slide one more time. But Fern, you really need to get this figured out."

"Yes, sir." My voice cracked, vision blurring for a second. "Thank you."

The rest of my shift was a flurry of rushing around, taking orders, and cleaning tables as a silent apology for my fumble.

So much for being slower than usual. Although it was busier than I'd expected for late afternoon, I could at least pour my nervous energy into the work. The other waitress, Candy, kept giving me strange looks.

When the crowd thinned, she met me behind the counter and put a hand on my shoulder. "You don't look so great. Are you getting sick?"

I shifted beneath her searching gaze. "No, I'm just a little tired."

Biting her lip, she tapped a manicured nail against her flawless cheek. "You should get some concealer for those dark circles. It might even make the blue in your eyes pop."

I smiled at her attempt at making me feel better. "Thanks, Candy, but I don't have time for makeup."

Her fist came to rest on one hip, and she arched a thin eyebrow. "Well, at least remember to pull your hair up for work." The fashionista scurried away to fill an order.

Shaking my head, I reluctantly bound my tangles up into a messy bun and returned to my own duties. I lost myself in the work, ignoring the customers' whispers behind my back.

But Tristan was more than happy to supply a suggestion. <*Those people are laughing at you. Maybe you should explain about the shifting tower.*>

When I was younger, I would have agreed. As a young teen, I managed to ignore him. But lately, his teasing banter held a thread of urgency that I couldn't ignore. Not to mention the elements of his world that kept leaking into my everyday life.

Shaking off the shiver that crept up my spine, I muttered, "Just be quiet…"

"What did you say?"

I spun around to find Candy staring at me.

"I was only asking if you could get the corner booth. But if you're going to be that way…" She stalked toward a man sitting alone at the farthest table in the small diner.

"Candy, wait—" I tried to take a deep breath, but my lungs felt heavy.

I can do this. I need to. For Elinore.

A buzzing in my pocket had me digging out my phone. One look at the name on the screen, and I rolled my eyes.

Yeah, no thanks, Dr. Richards. Today is definitely

not a day I want to talk to my shrink about.

I let the call go to voicemail, knowing he'd call back after I got off. I'd still ignore him.

Focused on working as quickly as I could to make up for my blunders, I scurried to clear the table nearest me. By the time my shift finally ended, my fingers burned and my feet ached.

I dodged out of the diner, my heart sighing with relief the minute my feet hit the sidewalk. The soft hum of people bustling through the stores slowed my racing pulse as the warmth of a hundred different lives wrapped around me. Each with his or her own worries and joys that dwarfed my insecurities, reminding me why I hadn't been too reluctant to give up driving.

Walking did something for my spirits. There were times when stretching my legs felt less like a freedom than a chore. But with metal beams launching food onto customers, forget driving.

A cold wind swept past, chilling me through my thin jacket and toying with the hem of my uniform. I could almost feel the touch of fingers at my elbow, but I shoved my arms tighter against my chest and kept walking.

Scurrying over the golden stars inlaid in the sidewalk, the clap-flap of my tennies sounded as hollow as I felt. The presumptuous Hollywood Stars were far grimier and uninteresting than anyone cared to admit, especially in this downtown area.

I reached the bus stop around the next bend just a few minutes before the 4:15 arrived. The folding door clicked open, and I slipped inside. After scanning my pass and offering the driver a quick smile, I shuffled to an empty row, choosing a seat near the window.

Settling into the chair, I smoothed out my dress and toyed absently with the mint-green pleats. While itching to try on the pair of jeans I'd scored at Goodwill the day before, I didn't really mind wearing the soft, '80s-style uniform.

Then again, my heart had always wrapped itself around vintage things. Being much too fond of Bing Crosby, Humphrey Bogart, and dainty folds of lace to fit in among most of my high-school classmates, I'd been beyond ready to graduate. Not that I'd been given the chance.

By freshman year, my concentration problems grew so bad that I couldn't even finish high school. The teachers had been hesitant to take on a student with my "mental needs," as they called them.

The chair beside me creaked, and I felt a soft nudge against my shoe. Tilting my head slightly, I could just make out Tristan's translucent blue sleeve touching my arm.

My stomach contorted. "You should go."

<There was a time when you would have saved me a seat.>

I gulped, trying to steady my voice. "That's before I was declared legally insane because of you. Before I failed high school and had to get a nine-to-five job and a tiny apartment. Before you ruined my life."

The vehicle's walls started to press in on me. Shifting in my seat, I stared out the window as the bus began to move.

<For the record, your job is eight to four. And none of that is my fault.>

I spun to glare at his flickering image. "Right, because you're a figment of my imagination." The words came out sharper than I intended. Unable to bear the strained look on his face, I studied the woven, padded, navy-blue armor he always wore. It seemed

22

THE GIRL WHO COULD SEE

more threadbare and faded now. "And yet, somehow, you still manage to wreck my life."

Tilting toward the window, I let my fingertips trail along the cool glass, distractedly watching the businesses blur by. Like most of the west LA and Hollywood area, the buildings were brightly colored and extravagant. Windows were filled with nostalgic posters, and broad lights rimmed many of the edges.

<I'm just trying to help.> Tristan sighed. <Fern, there's more going on here than you realize. Please. I need you to trust me like you used to.>

I can't listen to this. I huddled farther away from him, raising my hands to cover my ears. It just makes the hallucinations—the insanity—worse.

Chapter Three

His words trailed off, and he looked away. Sighed.

<Fern, I'm just trying to protect you.>

Please. Protect me right into a straight jacket.

Leaning forward, Tristan slipped something out of the ragged pack at his back. Two handles, wood wrapped in leather, with bent chains dangling from the tips. Each trail of links led to a round metal ball covered in spikes.

A flail.

One of my few history classes finally offered up some useful information.

It was a weapon.

The knowledge should have worried me, but I was

strangely unaffected. It felt so…natural. As if Tristan had always held those weapons, always run his callused fingers over their grips. They were a part of him.

No, there's nothing natural about him. Don't do this again—don't get attached.

Sighing, I turned back to the window, letting the scenery stream past but hardly registering what I was seeing.

Suddenly, a flash of glossy black feathers caught my eye. A sparrow. Its wings were spread out, catching a gust of wind and bobbing through the air. It spiraled, beat its wings a few times, and then came to rest on the top of a streetlight. Half a second later, though, it changed its mind. The small bird launched back into the air and flew in the opposite direction, the warm sun making its sleek feathers shine.

What I wouldn't give to be free like that…

To spread my wings and defy gravity. To know that no matter where I land, the world can't hold me there. That nothing can hold me down. Not even the weight in my chest or the gravity of their opinions.

<You'd better start smiling before you pick up

your niece, or she'll be worried.>

If I had to have an imaginary friend, couldn't it be one who didn't thrive on being my mother?

I turned back to Tristan and gave him the slightest nod. Shaking off the chilling cobwebs that had wound spindly fingers around my heart, I pulled out the ponytail holder that barely managed to keep my frizzy hair in place and let my knotted mane spill to my shoulders. I finger-combed it in an attempt to look more presentable. After twisting it up into another messy bun, I tied it back and tucked a stray auburn curl behind my ear.

He stowed the weapon again as the bus pulled up to the stop. *<Good luck.>*

Taking a deep breath, I plastered on a smile and stood. I ignored the brush of knees as I shuffled past the bench seats and filed off of the bus with the other passengers, determined to regain my composure.

Sand 'n' Sea Daycare was only a block from the bus stop and even closer to Elinore's school. Not wanting to make her wait any longer, I nearly ran all the way to the small building. I slipped through the big, overly cheery blue doors, signed in at the front desk, and waited while the clerk called for Elinore to meet me at the front.

Even though we were a good several miles away from the beach, the daycare's ocean-themed decorations warranted the name. Colorful starfish and seashells perched on shelves, and crashing waves were painted on the walls.

The small huddle of waiting mothers looked more put together than I'd felt in years. But at least the strange glances they'd given me when I started picking up Elinore had faded.

They never asked questions, so I never had to explain why I was functioning as Elinore's parent— why my sister had decided to carry on in the tradition of my mother with a too-small house that was too full of kids for any of them to really be taken care of. Or loved.

And how I'd offered to take Elinore, my sister's middle child, because I'd been desperately afraid she'd suffer the same childhood I'd had: practically invisible, hardly more than a mouth to feed.

When I disappeared at the age of eight, my parents hadn't noticed for three days. They gave up looking after twenty-four hours. They were far too busy trying to hide their stash of drugs when the authorities came knocking, investigating my absence.

My father was still serving jail time for that stunt—though his incarceration had been reduced due to my parents' compliance in the search. Even so, no one could find the child who'd been in a hospital one minute and gone the next.

A symphony of small footsteps interrupted my dark thoughts, and I looked up to find a stream of small bodies racing into the crowded room. I spotted Elinore's yellow blouse. Her tiny arms waved madly as fiery ringlets bounced about her shoulders.

"Aunt Fern!" she called, throwing herself into my arms.

I nuzzled her soft shoulder. "Hello there, darling. Did you have a good day?"

Her eyes twinkled up at me. "Oh, yes! My teacher says I'm a 'most creative student.'"

A chuckle bubbled out of me. "I can't imagine where you get that."

Her silvery giggle joined mine, and I glanced over her shoulder, pleased to find she'd remembered to grab her backpack. Taking her hand, I thanked the women at the checkout counter. Their tattoos matched their jewelry better than my rumpled attempts at fashion ever went together.

I escorted Elinore out of the building. Her voice dropped to a whisper as we stepped into the street. "Is *he* here?"

"El, I've told you, I'm not going to talk about him anymore. He's not real."

Her mouth puckered to the side, but she didn't press the issue. I balanced her pink lunch box in one hand and kept my other hand on her shoulder as I guided her down the sidewalk toward the bus stop. She dragged her feet when we passed a small cupcake shop, big eyes riveted on the iced delicacies in the window display.

"I wish we could, El, but we need to get home." Not to mention how tragically light my wallet was feeling at the moment.

At the bus stop, the vehicle was just slowing to a standstill when I caught sight of a blue-black uniform rounding the corner. A cop.

"Elinore, get on the bus *now*." I pushed her up the

steps, scanned my pass, and found us seats in the very back, away from any windows. I waited, knee jogging in rapid rhythm.

I have to be more careful. The last thing I needed was a police officer looking into my relationship with Elinore, or finding out how illegal it was for a nineteen-year-old with psychosis to be taking care of a child.

I'd already been questioned once by the cops patrolling this area, and they didn't need any more run-ins with the crazy girl who'd wrapped her car around a tree when a nonexistent building sprang up in the road.

The thrum beneath my feet and the gentle tug pressing me into my chair indicated the bus was on the move. I took a deep breath, relief settling over me like a cool breeze.

Clearing my throat, I glanced at my niece. "Are you hungry? I can get us a snack when we get home."

She shrugged. "I'm fine. Do you want to hold Clara?" She brought two small dolls out of her backpack and held one out to me.

After smoothing out the doll's blond tangles with

my fingers, I attempted to braid its hair, then passed the tiny figure back to Elinore. She spent the rest of the ride playing quietly. One doll sat on Elinore's lap while the other served the first doll imaginary food.

Her plaything had the same job I did. I made a mental note to create a waitress uniform for it when I could afford material. My arm draped around her thin shoulders as I watched her play, holding tightly to the one person who saw me as more than a broken piece in need of fixing.

We reached our bus stop in south LA and set out down the dirty side streets. As I rounded a corner, my vision blurred slightly, and I saw some sort of flight craft tilted on its side. Sand spilled out through broken windows as the rusted, dented vehicle sank into the piles of dust surrounding it.

I bit back a gasp at the sudden intrusion that was clearly not a part of the alley.

A network of pulsing blue wires snaked across the plane's wings, disappearing inside the angular cockpit. This had to be one of the flyers I'd heard Tristan mention.

I blinked several times, and the strange vision

disappeared.

I did it!

Allowing myself a victorious smirk, I picked up the pace, ignoring an odd look from Elinore.

In a few steps, we reached our apartment complex. Its two stories stretched out in an elongated rectangle, with doors set at random intervals. Rusted stairs spouted from the weary asphalt, leading from the main floor to the doors on the second. Shoddy, but it was a roof over our heads.

<*You know, you can't keep ignoring me.*> Tristan's voice barged uninvited into my thoughts, balling into a heavy weight in my chest.

I glanced down at Elinore. What I was about to do would undoubtedly give my shrink heart palpitations, but there had to be a way to banish the insanity lapping at the fraying edges of my mind. If losing him meant keeping Elinore…well, there was no contest.

"Hey, El, why don't you go up to your room? There's something I've got to deal with." I dropped the key in her hand.

"Oh-kaaay." Her feet pitter-pattered up the creaking steps to the door of our small apartment. She paused to glance at me, and I flashed her an encouraging smile till she moved inside.

I turned to confront my stalker. My eyes met his dark ones, and I felt a jolt of electricity from the impossible connection.

<That's better. Now, you have to listen to—>

"Just stop, all right? I have to ignore you. It's the only way to avoid a straitjacket and a windowless white room. Besides, you're only a coping mechanism to deal with what happened when I was younger."

I leveled my gaze at the flickering image in front of me. Tristan stood a good few inches taller than me, although he seemed to shrink a little every year. When I was a child, he'd been a giant. Now, as I surveyed his odd clothing—miscellaneous pieces of leather, metal, and unfamiliar materials sewn into a type of armor—he looked far less intimidating. "You aren't real."

Tangled, dusty-blond hair veiled searing blue eyes. Blue like mine but darker. Bearing vivid scars in their almost-black depths. I shivered, wondering what horrors could have caused that gaze to shift from gentle and teasing one moment to broken and haunting the next.

I had to stop thinking of him like that. He wasn't real. He didn't have a story of his own. Only what I'd given him.

Tristan took a wavering step nearer, and I stiffened.

<That's your shrink talking, Fern. C'mon, you've always known the truth. Ever since you were eight years old, I've been here to help you.>

Eight. When I disappeared. That only further proved he was the result of trauma. A figment of my imagination.

I glanced around the sidewalk in front of the apartment. Shadowed as it was, the last thing I needed were passersby reporting my shouting match in an empty alley.

I shook my head. "Please, just leave me alone."

I tried to walk away, but he dodged in front of me.

<It's not a game, Fern.> The gravity in his voice rooted me to the spot. *<You may never see me the way you did as a kid, but I can't wait for our bond to strengthen. There isn't time. The Rhoon has started clawing at the rift, and it's slowly getting through. The rift is widening, and your stubbornness is going to get*

us all killed.>

"Stubbornness?" My blood raged in my ears. While most of what he'd said made no sense, that word was painfully clear. "You think I'm being stubborn, trying to have a life? To protect Elinore? To not be locked up because of this insanity?"

Tristan's hands rose, palms up. *<I didn't mean—>*

"You know what? I'm done." Shoulders back, I took a step closer, glaring till he came into focus. "I'm not willing to lose everything I care about over the ravings of a hallucination."

<You have to believe me! If you don't, it will destroy everyone you love.>

"You're doing that just fine by yourself." Curling my fists, I stared at him till he was crisp, Technicolor, with a flicker around the edges of his form. "Good-bye, Tristan."

I strode right through him, and he vanished in a ripple of electricity. My skin felt clammy, chilled, but I made my way up the stairs and through the door Elinore had unlocked.

Kicking off my shoes, I stepped into the kitchen. I paused to listen, expecting to hear his muffled footsteps or steady breathing.

Nothing.

Had he really left? That had never happened before, no matter how much I'd ignored him.

I'd wanted him gone. But now that he was, I felt strangely empty.

Shaking off the unease raising goose bumps on my arms, I slid past the tiny card table flanked by two mismatched chairs. Elinore's small voice filtered through the adjoining bedroom, and I moved into the thin hallway. I strode across the ragged carpet, dodging the stacks of children's books. A stray Lego crunched under my heel.

I peeked into the room El and I shared to find her lying on her stomach on the bed, ankles crossed in the air behind her. She'd turned on the small television, navigating through the five channels we received to find PBS Kids. She grinned as she sang along with a catchy theme song.

I tapped the flip phone on her small dresser. "Hey, don't forget this next time you go to school. You never know when I may need to get ahold of you—or vice versa."

"Yup," she mumbled absently, and I pressed a kiss to her forehead.

"I'm going to take a quick shower, then I'll make us something to eat." Shower. Food. Two blissfully normal things.

She nodded without turning, thoroughly immersed in her show. I stepped into the attached bathroom, nudged aside a small pile of laundry to close the door, and washed my hands, careful not to splash water on the hair ties and faded jewelry cluttering the countertop.

As I twisted to grab a clean towel, my foot caught on Elinore's small wooden footstool. I went down. My elbows and knees smacked the floor hard enough to rouse bruises.

I looked up from where I lay sprawled on the linoleum, confusion spinning my thoughts.

He didn't catch me.

I couldn't remember the last time I'd actually fallen.

Brushing myself off, I rose to my feet. I opened the bathroom door and scanned the bedroom, where Elinore still lay on the hastily made twin bed surrounded by stacks of unpacked boxes, scattered toys, and piles of folded laundry.

Relief rose in my chest when I caught sight of Tristan leaning nonchalantly against the far wall, watching me through cool eyes. But the taut lines pulling at the edge of his smirk gave away the underlying tension.

<I can't leave you for one minute without you hurting yourself, can I?>

"What, you only help me when you feel like it?"

His finger wagged. *<That's the one room I don't follow you into. Unless you'd prefer...>*

As his meaning dawned on me, my eyes grew big. I didn't know whether to be relieved or angry with myself for never considering that aspect of his protective presence. "How long has that been a boundary?"

He shrugged. *<Since I first met you. I'm your friend. Not some perv.>*

I'd never thought he was.

No longer interested in a shower, I went to the bed and squeezed Elinore's shoulder. "I think I'll make us something to eat now."

She nodded, and I suddenly realized she'd ignored my one-sided conversation with Tristan as if it were natural.

Pressing fingertips to the headache building in my temples, I made my way back to the kitchen, limping a bit. The pile of souring dishes on the counter reminded me I'd been falling behind on my chores. I needed something to do with my hands while I sorted through my warring emotions.

Before I could start the hot water, a pair of strong hands settled on my shoulders.

<How did you do that? Block me out?> Tristan's warm breath grazed my ear.

"I don't know." My headache continued to throb, heightened by the confusion I felt at Tristan's odd presence. "But I'm beginning to wish it had lasted longer." I pressed my palms flat on the counter and tilted my head toward the ghost standing beside me.

<Everything you're seeing is real, Fern. I can show you what's really going on if you'll let me.>

"No." The word, hardly more than a whisper, spoke of a decade of desperation.

He let go of me and backed away. *<Fern.>* He

tapped a fist against the thin scar lacing his jaw. *<I'm not doing this. The rift is.>*

A hiccupped sob escaped my tightly closed lips. He'd used that word before, but I'd never asked what it meant. "Rift?"

<Something new is happening, and I think you're in danger.>

"Real danger?" I glanced at his armor again.

He moved an inch closer. *<The rift is a breach between my world and yours. The fabric of space and time separating our two worlds has torn. Somehow, you are able to see both sides.>*

I forgot to breathe.

The messy apartment I stood in disappeared, replaced by ancient buildings sprawled in a wasteland of dust and cobwebs. Rust and shadows hugged the shattered windows and gaping doorways. I could almost taste the stench of rotting flesh.

There was something strangely familiar about this place.

As suddenly as it appeared, the desolate scenery dissolved. Just like the dreams I'd harbored of a normal life.

Chapter Four

Present Time

Halting my narrative with a wave of his huge hand, the FBI agent narrows his eyes at me. "So, let me get this straight. You're telling me that your hallucinations are glimpses into another world?"

"A parallel world, to be exact."

Barstow blows out a long breath as he leans back in his chair. "I've read your file, Miss Johnson. I know you went missing when you were eight years old. And that it wasn't your parents who reported the disappearance—it was a worried neighbor who said she hadn't seen you playing with your siblings for almost a week. When the police got involved, they found out your parents had a side job—selling crack. And they were using their children to peddle it."

I cringe, the memories far from pleasant, but he plows ahead.

"Your parents claimed you'd cut your arm and they'd rushed you to a hospital. But there's no trace of you ever having been in the hospital. In fact, there was no trace of where you disappeared to at all. And three years later, you returned home, malnourished and covered in bruises, scars, and puncture wounds."

I lean back in my chair, resisting the urge to rub my fingertips along the inside of my wrists where faded scars had long served as a reminder of my absence.

Barstow cocks his head, his gray eyes ripping through me.

"You want to know what I think happened? I think your parents *sold* you. You were trafficked at the ripe young age of eight. But you managed to escape and find your way home. And all of the strange stories you told were just a way to deal with the horrible things that happened to you. It's a textbook case."

I shrug, curling the edge of my light-colored scarf

around a finger.

I've heard all this before. Believed it for years, because even trafficking seemed easier to swallow than the truth. But that didn't make what happened any less true. "You sound like my shrink."

His dark brows rise. "You're still seeing a therapist?"

"Of course. They're assigned to me by the state."

"Your records say you were suspended from court-appointed therapy for the next year." He doesn't sound convinced.

"What? I was suspended for a few months, but not a whole year. Must be a misprint."

He looks like he's about to press the issue, but I've been sidetracked long enough. I'm here to talk about the danger we're all in, not a filing mix-up with my psychiatrist.

"Look, even if your theory about my childhood disappearance is true, that doesn't explain how I knew about the building's collapse."

He rolls his eyes. "But an imaginary friend from another planet does?"

I exhale slowly. "Yeah, I didn't believe that when

I first heard it either."

Chapter Five

Ten Days Earlier

My body quivered as I turned the knobs on the kitchen sink. Cupping my hands beneath the stream, I splashed cool water in my face.

This can't be happening. What Tristan had just shown me had to be some kind of trick.

After grabbing a cup, I turned toward my tiny refrigerator and reached inside for a jug of cold water. Tristan appeared to my left. *<You left the water out this morning. I tried to tell you.>*

Filling the cup from the kitchen tap instead, I lifted it toward Tristan. "Cheers."

I needed to process all this, and I couldn't do that

if my thoughts weren't my own. So I dug the plethora of prescription drugs out of the cupboard, popped several pills into my mouth, and chased it with the water.

I expected Tristan to fire off another sarcastic comment. Instead he stared at me, his frown like granite.

I rubbed a palm against my thin dress, trying to generate some warmth. "Hey, don't be like that. It's not going to hurt you. You'll just...go away for a while."

He shook his head, blue eyes sparking like angry stars. Suddenly, he lurched toward me, clamped his hands on my shoulders, and pushed me back against the wall. His body was so close I could feel his chest heaving.

How was that possible?

<*You need to snap out of it. Everything they've told you is a lie. I'm not something you created. I'm real. More real than anything you've known.*>

"I know what you're doing. Dr. Richards said this might happen."

His brows furrowed. <*What did he say?*>

With my hands flat against his chest, I felt the kinks and slices in the worn armor that plated his firm torso.

"You're using alienation tactics. You want me to walk away from everything I know and be consumed by my own mind. To leave Elinore and this whole world. Well, it won't work."

Tristan raked his eyes across the ceiling as if searching for answers written there.

<I would never want to take you away from Elinore. Or the rest of your world. I'm not trying to lure you into some trap—I'm trying to save you. All of you. But if you keep pushing me away, you'll lose everything.>

His face was so near I could see every jagged detail in the faint scars lacing his skin.

<Earth will be destroyed.>

"How can you expect me to believe that?" I was balancing on the edge of a precipice. If I tipped off the ledge, would I find the answers I was desperate for— or be lost forever?

He shrugged his broad shoulders and rubbed a hand against a ridge in his armor. *<If you won't*

believe it for the good of your world...> He cocked his head to the side in that lost-puppy way he used to when I was young. *<Believe it for an old friend.>*

He stepped close again. With a tanned finger, he traced a line down the side of my face, warming my skin with his touch.

How can I possibly be feeling this?

<I saved you so many times as a child. From those men who took you and anyone else who meant you harm. It was easy for you to believe in me then. Why can't you now?>

"I don't know."

My breathing became labored again, but excitement raced through my veins. A familiar hope, long buried, unearthed by memories of the little girl he spoke of. I gulped, scrambling for the answers that had seemed so concrete only minutes ago. "I guess I grew up."

<Told you that was a mistake.>

I blew out a long breath, stifling the urge to nudge aside the tangle of hair that fell across one of his eyes. "Some of us aren't immortal."

Tristan barked a laugh, his face lighting up.

<Immortal?>

"Yeah, like you. You never age." The familiar banter was like a breath of air to aching lungs.

He chuckled. *<Next you'll say I have magic powers.>*

I glared at him. "You don't look any different to me than you did when I was eight."

<Time is different in our worlds, just as distance is. To me, I've only known you for a few years—to you, it's been a lifetime. I have been aging, it's just so gradual to you that you haven't noticed.>

"How old are you?"

<I was fifteen when we met. Now I'm almost twenty.>

I peered at him. "That means you're only a year older than I am."

He lifted a hand, palm flat. *<Plant Girl, can you believe in me just one more time?>*

My mind swirled with questions I hadn't dared to ask—until now. *What if I'm not insane—what if it's true? All of it?*

The repercussions of that statement were almost too much for me to process.

Realizing the refrigerator was still open, I closed the door and heard the solid *click* of the seal. The dog-eared drawing taped to the fridge was so familiar I hardly saw it anymore—a tall figure, clothed in the colors of a caped hero, my earliest memory of Tristan drawn unsteadily in red and blue crayon.

At the time, I'd been too young to understand that the crimson was blood, stained and dripping. It hadn't mattered anyway when he appeared inside the white room where the strange men kept me. His gentle voice washed away my fears.

And when he showed me how to escape—the right things to tell the woman when she visited again and which corners to turn as I fled the building—he had been more than a friend. He'd been my hero.

My parents thought that my love of the caped hero with powers was simple childlike imagination. They didn't know that I spoke to my rescuer every day. That he became my friend and protector. As I grew up, I learned his real name and a bit more about him. Tristan had always been my hero. And my best friend.

Until now.

<The Rhoon is trying to get through the rift, and

soon it will do to your world what it's done to mine.>

I cleared my throat. "And what's that?"

Tristan looked away, his expression growing distant.

<Destroy it. I watched my entire race die in screaming agony. Watched our lush landscapes crumble to dust. I spent my nights cursing the air that still filled my lungs, wishing I could die too. You were the only light, after the Rhoon came. As a child, you were special to me. Someone to protect, to live for. But then I watched you grow up.>

His laugh had a note I couldn't quite understand. *<And you became something more.>*

My hand lingered on the picture, the waxy feel of crayon resting under my fingertips, but I was acutely aware of Tristan beside me.

Out of the corner of my eye, I watched him drag a knuckle across his face, removing some of the dirt and grime. He was actually quite handsome underneath all that. I'd never noticed it before. I'd been too busy trying to push him away.

<You were my saving grace. Someone I could talk to. Someone who understood being alone. You kept me

sane. You were my lifeline in a world that was dark and desolate.>

What a strange perspective. These last years, he'd been the embodiment of my lunacy. Yet I was his sanity.

Finally turning to face him, I found him reaching out his hand to me. His soft gaze drank in every detail of my face, holding me frozen in that one glance.

<I can't lose you now.>

With those words, something broke inside me. A carefully erected wall crumbled—a wall built to distance myself from everything Tristan was to me. To convince myself I didn't need him. Only, that was a lie. Tristan was the best thing that'd ever happened to me. Other than Elinore, he was the only person who'd never left. Never seen me as a demented, broken shell of a woman. The only person who hadn't given up on me.

I would be insane to walk away from a love like that.

"And I don't want to lose you." My hand slipped into his, and I stared at the place where his skin lay beneath mine, willing myself to feel it again. To feel him.

Like water beginning to flow over dry, cracked rocks, the feeling returned. His hand materialized under mine, callused and strong.

Real.

My gaze met his. "Tell me what's really going on."

<It's probably better that I show you.>

Chapter Six

Tristan dropped my hand and strode forward, walking through the wall of the kitchen like it didn't even exist. In his world, it didn't.

Rooted to my position beside the refrigerator, I watched as Tristan crossed what seemed to be a long distance. His feet worked quickly, sweat soaking his hair and rolling down his neck like he was in a steady run, caked in a haze of golden dust. But as I followed him out of the kitchen to peer from the open doorway, he seemed to only leave the apartment.

My eyes burned as they tried to make sense of two visions that refused to coincide—like having one eye nearsighted, the other farsighted, fighting two different perspectives of one image. I concluded that time must not be the only thing that passed differently between our two worlds. Depth and distance were incongruous as well. No wonder Tristan always seemed to be right behind me, no matter how far I went.

Tristan passed through the alley behind my apartment to duck around something I couldn't see before he finally stopped moving. The area around him solidified until only Tristan remained, hunched down on the asphalt and whispering for me to join him.

This is crazy!

Throwing on my shoes, I hesitantly descended the apartment's rusted steps. I knelt a few inches from Tristan, staring through the shadowed alley into what looked like a busy street.

<Do you remember how I said that my world was destroyed? That I'm the sole survivor?>

"Yes." The word seemed so insufficient. There were times when I'd felt alone, but an entire world of people still surrounded me. What Tristan meant…that was something else completely.

<This is why.>

I strained to see what he did, and suddenly, only feet ahead of me, was a lurking, monstrous presence. A creature of some kind—rock hard and towering over me like a shadow blotting out the sun. I couldn't breathe. My heart raced. Every instinct told me to run.

With a shriek, I scrambled backward, trying to put as much distance between me and that *thing* as I could.

<It's okay. It can't touch you. It's not in your world—yet.>

My shoulders stopped heaving as I finally caught my breath, Tristan's steady hand on my back. Letting my eyes slowly rise, I took in the scene once again.

Sand cloaked the broken world ahead of me—yet it wasn't sand. The golden flakes covered the craggy ground, withered plants, and bleached buildings, clinging like a sickness and leaching out any sense of vitality. An airborne disease that slinked into every crack and crevice. The minerals from the ground and buildings were inhaled by the dust, leaving behind a chalky, frail shell. The plants' strength and life sucked away. Shriveled.

My stomach recoiled. "What is that?"

<Death.>

Gritting my teeth and forcing myself not to move, I struggled to focus on what I was seeing. A heavy mist cloaked the narrow alley in front of me. The tail end of the apartment building and the surrounding pavement was no longer visible.

What the glistening dust revealed was certainly not Los Angeles. It clung to the ridges of a crumbling building, an ancient structure with so many gaping holes it resembled a skeleton. The building itself was haunting enough, but something seemed eerie and depressing about the glistening fog too. Something...unnatural.

<We called it Rhoon, the ancient word for death, since we did not know how else to describe it. When it first appeared, it was a light spray of dust, hardly enough to resemble a cloud. But it grew quickly once it started to feed.>

I gasped. "Feed? On what?"

His face paled, the scars standing out on his skin. *<Us. It infected the children first, then spread to the adults. We couldn't find a cure or a way to keep it out. The acid seeped through closed doors and shuttered windows, sucking the life from anything it touched.*

Once it finished with the people, it began to destroy the crops and anything that held minerals or any kind of vitality.>

My lips clenched between my teeth. I turned to look with new eyes at the crumbling buildings. They weren't only in disrepair; they were frail, bleached shells of what they had been.

I'd seen this place before. A long time ago, when the sun lit up the world and people moved about. When it thrived. Now it was a wasteland.

What was this monster that could desolate an entire planet?

And why hadn't Tristan been affected?

He practically read my mind. *<I was immune, somehow, to the disease. My father thought it was something genetic, but he didn't live long enough to discover the details.>* His face was drawn and shadowed. Broken.

"If you're immune, maybe there's a way to create a cure for the plague."

He looked at the buildings again, but this time with a small spark in those dark eyes. *<I don't think I'm immune in that sense. Personally, I think you're*

the reason the Rhoon couldn't poison me. Because of our bond, I'm connected to the rift. Which means that I'm not fully in this world or in yours. Being in between somehow makes it impossible for the Rhoon to infect me. But even so...> He turned toward me, his eyes hollow. *<It's not a plague. A plague cannot think; it cannot change form.>*

My attention snapped back to the glinting mist, wondering if I even wanted to be this close. "What do you mean?"

<It has two forms—one almost liquid, like sand, an airborne disease. The other a firm body. The mist can stabilize into something hard enough to split skin.>

With painful clarity, I counted the crisscrossing scars on his upper arm.

<When it realized it couldn't poison me, it grew more aggressive. It began to hunt.>

I took a step backward, the coarse feel of pavement beneath my shoes a welcome link to reality. "I can't stop something like that. I don't even know how I'd fight it!"

<You don't. Fighting it is no use—there's only

one way we can stop it. I think the Rhoon has nearly used up its entire food source in my world. If we can trap it here, it could starve to death.>

Now, that I might actually be able to do. If I can see through this rift into Tristan's world, maybe I can find a way to close that link. To cut off the Rhoon from Earth. But first... "We have to find a way to get you out of there. I'm not sealing that creature off until you're safely here, in this world."

My words were instinctive, a whiplash reaction that I didn't even pause to think through. That thing had nearly given me a heart attack, and I'd never seen it in its physical form—let alone spent years hunted by the monster. There was no way I'd leave him there alone with it.

Tristan stared at me for a long moment. *<You'd do that?>*

"Of course. Hallucination or not, I won't just leave you there to die." I knew what it was like to be trapped by a monster with no hope of escape—only my demons had worn lab coats instead of a hide of sand. Still, I hated bullies, no matter what shape they came in. I glanced over my shoulder at the Los

Angeles skyline. "We need to get you away from that world and into this one."

His laugh was dry. *<Getting me through is the least of your troubles. The Rhoon has used up this world and is in search of another feeding source. Now that the rift has widened...>*

A chill swept over me. Tristan had warned me so many times, and yet now that I fully understood the danger, it felt all the more real. The words left my lips, as if their release confirmed the Rhoon's arrival. "It's coming to Earth."

<Yes. And I know where it will break through next. But you don't have much time. Once the rift is open far enough, nothing can stop it.>

"Well, then it's about time we tell someone."

I spun away, heading back up the stairs.

<Where are you going?>

"To find some way to contact the FBI."

Chapter Seven

Present Time

In the silence that envelops the interrogation room, my racing heartbeat sounds like thunder. I shift in the hard seat, wincing when it lets out a *creak* that only makes Barstow's thick brows arch more as he leans over the table toward me. The otherwise-empty room is suddenly stifling.

The agent runs his large hand over his sparse scalp, lips pressed into a thin line. "Do you have any way to prove this insane story?"

My gaze drifts to where Tristan hovers behind the agent. His image has paled, and I squint, trying to solidify him. He disappeared for a few hours while I passed through several FBI screenings before making it to this room.

As I focus on Tristan, I realize he's clutching his side. A bead of crimson slides through his fingers. It hits the floor, a tiny red droplet staining the carpet.

"Miss Johnson?"

The agent's words bring my attention back to him—and cut through my confident facade. For the first time since I walked into this room, fear pierces my chest. Tristan is hurt, and if I can't make this man believe me, I'll be unable to do anything for him. If Barstow won't help me, I'll lose a lot more than just the city. I'll lose the very people who give me reason to keep living.

I ball my fists at my side. "If the rift has torn open large enough, there may be a way for you to see Tristan."

The agent's brows knit together as he glances around the room. "All right, where is he?"

I peek around his shoulder, but Tristan's disappeared again. And this time, he's wounded. I try to swallow the knot in my throat. "He was behind you, but now he's gone."

Agent Barstow snorts. "How convenient."

My scarf feels tight as a noose. "He's usually right behind me. I've never had to find him before. He always finds me. Please, let me look for him."

Barstow stands. "I'll be right back."

He exits through the door in the back of the room, most likely to talk to his superiors. Another agent, his curly dark hair slicked back, takes his place and watches me with intense emerald eyes.

I have to find a way out of here and get to Tristan. I'm so thankful Elinore is safely on a playdate at Mrs. Kent's house, probably enjoying the day off from school. I could never bring her into this.

"Can I use the restroom?"

"You have to stay here until Barstow returns. It won't be long."

Seconds later, Agent Barstow comes back. He nods to the younger agent. "Stand down, Amieer. She's been released."

A muscle in the man's clean-shaven jaw relaxes as he steps away from the door, gesturing to me.

Pushing my chair back from the table, I slowly rise to my feet. Arms crossed, I peer at Barstow skeptically. "You're letting me go? Just like that?"

"We have no cause to detain you."

That can only mean... "You don't believe me."

He shakes his head and disappears out the door. The remaining agent steers me down countless hallways, where I receive hostile glances from men and women bustling about in pristine business suits.

When we reach the exit at the front of the large building, I pause to stare up at the FBI headquarters. When I entered this fortress, I'd hardly been able to keep my knees from shaking. Now that I've made it out, the mystery dissipated, I feel empty. Nothing has changed. I'm no closer to saving my friend or my world.

I walk across the street and make my way toward the bus stop, my stomach so twisted I'm not sure how long I'll keep my breakfast down.

Where would I even start to look for Tristan?

My pulse freezes in my veins as a glimmer of crimson on the asphalt catches my attention. Blood. Just like in the interrogation room.

I try to strengthen my view into Tristan's world. Dust coats everything—the strange plague that has demolished his planet and is ready to do the same to mine.

The dribble of blood gives way to a trail of drops. I break into a run, following the path.

"Tristan! Where are you?"

<*Over here.*> His voice is husky like he's in pain.

My throat tightens as I dodge down a side street, racing toward the front of a restaurant. The establishment wavers like a mirage before my eyes, one minute a construct of chipping red paint, the next a haze of golden dust burying some kind of cement slab. Tristan is the only constant. He lies on the pavement in front of the restaurant—or the dust-covered slab—tilted on his side, eerily transparent. Crimson spreads around him like a sheet of ice.

My knees slam to the sidewalk, but I don't feel it. I stare at the massive gash that tears along his rib cage, cutting through the makeshift armor to reveal raw flesh. A flash of white—possibly bone.

"Quick! Someone call an ambulance!"

People spin in my direction, their faces showing concern but also confusion. That's right—they can't see him. From their perspective, I'm kneeling on the sidewalk, talking to empty air.

<Forget the ambulance. It won't do any good. They can't reach through to me. I'm going to have to sew up the wound myself.>

I nearly lose my meal. *He's going to stitch himself up? Without pain meds or a first-aid kit?*

A low chuckle parts his chapped lips as a playful gleam fills his eyes. *<Don't worry. I've dealt with this before.>*

Peeking around, I wish I were as invisible as Tristan. If I try to help him here, in clear view of passersby, it won't take long for someone to alert the authorities of the deranged teenager mumbling to herself.

What am I thinking? My best friend is bleeding out, and I'm worried about looking bad?

Then again, isn't that how I've always responded? Like he's just a nuisance? While he's been trying to save the world, I've been too consumed with keeping up appearances.

Well, that stops today.

As my determination overtakes my fear, Tristan's world invades my own. The restaurant is still in view, but the building behind it fades to a charred landscape. I reach down, helping him unhook his armor and slide the bloody wrappings away.

Setting the interwoven plates of metal and leather beside me, I tear off my beige scarf and press the balled-up material against his bleeding wound. Lying there in his worn brown tunic without his armor, he looks less like a warrior and more like a boy—a boy who is squinting and biting his lip in a ridiculously charming way.

I shake away my tangled emotions and keep pressure on the wound, watching as the blood slows to a halt. "Do you make it a habit to get speared?"

<Clawed, actually. I was following the Rhoon to find out where the breach was, but it saw me and wasn't happy.>

He's carrying on a conversation. That's a good sign. His recklessness, however, isn't. "That was stupid, Tristan. You should have waited."

I need to keep him talking. Coherent. "How is the rift in one physical spot if I'm seeing through it everywhere?"

<Somehow, you are connected to the rift. You can

expand and narrow it, no matter where you are. But the focal point, the incision, the puncture wound in your world—that's a stable place. A physical tear in the fabric of space and time. That's where the Rhoon is trying to get through—>

His reply is cut off by a shout at my back. I swivel, watching the dust around me fade into the LA street. The businesses lining the sidewalks have emptied out, the rows of parked cars replaced by one large black SUV, its door open. Agents funnel out of it. An ambulance, siren blaring, pulls into a parking spot.

A group of men in dark slacks and vests with *FBI* emblazoned on them in yellow run toward me, trailed closely by two EMTs carrying medical equipment. I wave a frantic hand at Agent Barstow, who heads the pack.

"What's going on here?" Barstow's steady gait slows as he nears. "Is that blood?"

He's still as detached as he was in the interrogation room, but there's a curious light in his eyes. His dark skin has a slight flush, and his brow is rippled in concentration. He barrages me with questions, quick and methodical. As if he can piece together—and do something about—what most other men would miss.

I have a suspicion that's why he followed me here, even though he clearly didn't believe me in the interrogation. Barstow is a man of action.

If I'm going to convince him of Tristan's existence, I need to speak his language. I have to show him something tangible. Sidling back from my crouched position beside Tristan, I answer, "It's not my blood. Here—let me show you."

Still holding onto Tristan, I reach toward the agent, palm up. An invitation. A last resort.

After three stretching seconds, a callused hand takes my small one, and my eyes clamp closed. I focus all my strength on Tristan, trying to solidify whatever strange bond we have. Delving into the impossible that I've pushed away for so long—embracing it. Letting the strange electricity flow from him into me. Like swimming downward, fighting a current, I push into his world. Expanding what I can see.

A warm breeze and grainy bits of sand pelt my skin. Dust leaks beneath my knees as I give in to the impossible. And bend the tear in our worlds to my will.

I keep my eyes closed, afraid to let anything shatter this moment, even as the sensations of his world wrap around me—and hopefully around Barstow.

A strangled cough and muttered expletive are proof that it does. "What the—"

Barstow's hand grows slick in my grasp, but he doesn't let go. Not until I do.

The connection severed, Tristan's world recedes. But I hang on to the young man, keeping him steady till he's visible in my world. The landscape behind him fades out of view, replaced by the arching city skyline. His image stops wavering.

I've never tried holding him in my world for this long. But maybe I can keep him stationary long enough for Barstow and the medical personnel to help him.

The lines of pain in Tristan's face make my chest ache. I can hear a soft *plop-plop-plop* as his blood runs off the sidewalk, dripping into a gutter.

Agent Barstow's hands sink to his sides. "I-I can't

believe it."

He sees him. He *sees* Tristan.

My throat is tight as my eyes brim with tears. I'd almost given up hope anyone would ever believe me...

The blood pooling around Tristan pulls me into focus. Spinning toward the agent, I lift my chin. "Sir, you saw his world. That's what will become of ours if we don't find a way to stop it. But first, Tristan needs medical aid."

My pulse pounds a rhythmic plea in my ears. *Please help us...please help us...please help us...*

He straightens, tugging on the edge of his coat. "All right. You have me convinced that there's more to you than a psychotic breakdown." His tone shifts to stern and commanding, and he gives rapid-fire instructions to the EMTs before he turns back to me. "When I saw blood on the floor of the interrogation room, I thought it was yours."

He saw it too?

I turn to stare at Tristan, whose face reflects the shock I feel. "How is this possible?"

<It's your link to me. Somehow you strengthened it enough for Barstow to catch a glimpse, even without

realizing it.>

The EMTs step forward, one carrying a large first-aid kit.

Thank God.

"Can you reach him?" I take Tristan's limp hand.

The other EMT nods slowly as he bends down beside me. He presses a hand against Tristan's waist, slightly above the gaping wound. Tristan gasps, wrenching sharply.

<I felt that.> His wild eyes capture mine. *<I've never been able to interact with anyone but you.>*

I can't tell if the tears glimmering in his eyes are from disbelief or pain, but I squeeze his hand tighter. "Does this mean the rift is widening?"

He sucks in a ragged breath. *<Could be. Though whether that's because of you or the Rhoon, I'm not sure.>*

He lurches again when the EMTs remove my bloodstained scarf and poke the red, inflamed flesh around the wound.

My stomach constricts, and I must look about how I feel, because Barstow takes a step closer.

"Is everything okay?"

<She has a thing about medical procedures and blood. Being kept in a lab for years will do that to you.>

I try to ignore Tristan's words, but Barstow insists I translate, so I do.

"...but I'll be fine." I quickly add. "Let me know how I can help."

Barstow turns back to the EMTs. "How are we doing? Can you patch him up?"

The older EMT rubs a fist against the light stubble peppering his chin. "I'm not even sure what it is I'm seeing..."

Barstow glares at him.

"Right. No questions asked." He trades a long look with the EMT clutching the first-aid kit. "Under normal circumstances, we'd take him back to a hospital to stabilize him. Stop the bleeding, stitch him up, and give him a blood transfusion. But I'm assuming we can't move him?"

Tristan and I shake our heads.

The EMT nods. "We'll do what we can here then. After I stop the bleeding, we'll clean the wound."

"How can I help?"

"Keep him talking. Distracted."

While the medical personnel press the sides of the wound together, applying pressure with strips of towels to stop the flow of blood, I try to start up a conversation. His dialogue is stunted with groans, but I can tell he's trying.

"Tell me something about your world. The way it used to be. What do you miss the most?"

His face has paled considerably. *<Other than the people? I think I miss the birds.>*

His attention shifts to something over my shoulder, and I glance back to see a flock of sparrows perched on the roof of one of the nearby buildings.

"Really? Why?"

<They're just so...alive.> He pauses to clench his jaw as the EMTs begin to clean the wound. When he can finally speak, his voice is strained. *<When you're the only sane creature left on your planet, you start to miss that. The carefree weightlessness of simply being alive. The birds don't live nearly as long as we do, and yet not once do they ever worry if they're doing enough. They just are. Not held down by anything.>*

"They're free." My voice shakes.

The lines threading his forehead smooth for a moment. *<Exactly.>*

"Here." One of the EMTs leans closer, handing Tristan a few pills. He downs all of them before they can offer him water. Shaking his head, the man surveys the other ragged scars lacing my friend's chest. "This doesn't seem to be the first time you've been injured like this. Who sewed up the other incisions?"

<I did,> Tristan coughs out, and I relay to the EMTs, who share a shocked look. Without another word, they set about cleaning the wound. The muscle in Tristan's jaw clenches. Looks like the painkillers aren't much help.

Barstow tries to talk to me, but I shake my head. "Not now. Sorry, but I have to concentrate."

The EMTs murmur to each other for a few minutes, then glance between Tristan and me. "It's time to stitch him up."

My stomach drops. *I don't want to have to watch this...* "Maybe we should try getting him to a hospital, after all?"

Tristan lifts his head and grips my hand tighter.

<Trust me, I can handle this. I rescued you from that lab and beat off bullies when you were in middle school. Compared to that, a little needle is nothing.>

His jokes are meant to ease my fear, but something in my chest coils tighter. Before I can dissuade him, Tristan faces the emergency medical technicians. *<Do it.>*

Although they can't hear him, his intention is clear. A sterile needle and a length of thread make me look away. I'm surprised I haven't already fainted. "Tristan …"

<I'll be fine, Plant Girl. Don't worry.>

Right. Nothing to worry about. You're just bleeding all over a sidewalk, and in minutes I'll have to let you return to the world where a monster tore you to shreds.

His thumb makes a few slow circles on the back of my hand until my eyes meet his. He mouths a wordless, *Thank you.*

The first EMT passes Tristan a thin piece of wood to chomp down on. The other places gloved hands on either side of the gash, pressing the flayed edges together.

"Let's do this."

Chapter Eight

Tristan grinds his teeth into the wooden tongue depressor between his lips. Even the FBI agents clustered around us hold their breaths as the EMTs do their job.

My friend doesn't make a sound as the needle and thread drag through the raw flesh, binding up the wound. But there's a rigid set to his jaw, and his usually vivid gaze is filmy.

What he must have endured to survive all those years alone. Or mostly alone.

No, I left him alone.

A chill spiderwebs up my arms. I rejected him.

Time and time again, I pushed him away when all he wanted was someone to listen. I spent so much time looking up to him, needing him, rejecting him—but not once had I ever truly been there *for* him. Not in the way he was for me.

I turn away, unable to watch. Guilt hardens in my chest.

His fingers tremble in my hand, and I blink back the wetness gathering in my eyes. I wrap both hands around Tristan's free one, trying to pour my warmth into his chilled skin.

<F-Fern?>

His voice is weak, almost feverish. And he didn't call me *Plant Girl.*

"I'm here." I blink as his eyes focus on my face. "I'm not going anywhere." My voice breaks on the last word, but I've never meant it more.

I keep Tristan distracted, asking him questions as the EMT ties off the stitches. After wiping the area with antiseptic one last time, the uniformed man wraps white gauze around Tristan's chest. Tristan pulls down his shirt, and the EMT backs away, hands full of bloody towels.

"I suggest he rest for at least a few hours, if not days, to let the wound heal," the other EMT says. "The wound will need to be cleaned regularly and the bandages changed to prevent infection."

<Thanks for patching me up,> Tristan says, and I parrot his words back to them, *<but I'll have to take that break some other time.>* Shaking, he rises to his feet. Still holding my hand, he makes eye contact with Agent Barstow. *<We have to find the rift.>*

Barstow waves away the EMTs. They carry their supplies back to the ambulance.

Slipping my arm around Tristan's waist, careful not to touch his bandage, I move with him a few steps away where he can sit somewhere that's not covered in blood. I sway on my feet, light-headed. My energy must be sapped from maintaining such a deep connection with him for so long.

When Tristan takes his arm from across my shoulders, sinking into a sitting position, he fades back into the translucent state I'm so familiar with.

I take slow, deep breaths, trying not to let him see my exhaustion. "Are we going to try to find the rift again?"

His hand hovers over his ribs, lightly brushing the thick bandages bulging through his armor. <*I know where it is on my side, but it'll be difficult to find it on yours. That's why we have to start looking right away.*>

"And once we find it…do you know how to close it?"

His eyes are glued to the ground. <*Maybe. I'll know once we get there.*>

That's strangely vague for someone who's been preparing years for this moment.

"Where do you think you're going?" Agent Barstow grabs my arm and spins me around to face him. "I'm putting my team on finding that rift, and I'm sending you to the nearest hospital for an exam."

"What? Why?" A crowd stands several feet away, but I ignore the hardly contained whispers and pointing fingers. It's nothing new.

He drops my arm. "To prove that you're not insane."

He's still regarding me with that granite stare. But no longer does he look at me like I'm some poor, withered creature who's too fragile to survive.

Now I'm a means to an end. I'm the girl who can see through worlds and may actually be on to something. I'll take that over *broken* any day. "That...boy...said that you were at a lab. I want to know what they did to you and what it has to do with the threat."

The thought of finally having answers both thrills and terrifies me. With every fiber of my being, I want to close the rift and finally have Tristan—and everyone I care about—safe. But if we have to dig into my childhood to do it...

I buried those memories for a reason. And I don't know what I'll find if I dredge them up again.

I'm not given much choice in the matter, though. Two FBI agents lead me toward the waiting ambulance. Sighing, I follow along, dragging my feet. Rising with a groan, Tristan limps alongside me. "You're the one who should be going to a hospital. You can hardly walk."

<I can keep up—distance is different between our two worlds, remember? It won't be as far for me.>

"You broke into a sweat just crossing my apartment."

<Yes, but it's not all linear like that. The distance won't always be farther on my side than on yours. It just depends on where we're going.>

"I'm not sure I followed any of that, but I'll take your word for it. Do you really think we can afford to waste time on some tests, though? Shouldn't we focus on finding the rift?"

<Whatever they did to you in that lab is somehow tied in to our connection and the rift itself. I can't give you any real answers—but maybe these doctors can. If there's a chance that learning more about your connection can help us shut down the rift, then we should definitely take it.>

I shudder at his mention of the lab I was trapped in for three years, then glance at the agents flanking me. "I've been told two different stories about my disappearance my whole life. Both are like horror movies. I'm not sure if I really want to know what happened in that lab."

We've almost reached the ambulance when Tristan sighs. *<This is not something you can ignore. Somehow, someday, you're going to have to face it.>*

I shake my head and rub the bridge of my nose.

"There's a whole lot more at stake here than just my happiness, so I'll let the doctors do whatever tests they want and answer any questions they have. But after that, we save the world. And then we move on, okay?"

A little color returns to his face as he winks. *<When all this is over, I'd be more than happy to move on with you.>*

I roll my eyes and climb into the passenger seat of the ambulance cab while the EMT and two agents hop in the back. Barstow fills the driver in on our destination: the Jefferson-Davies Medical Center.

The vehicle slides forward, and the pungent odors of the ambulance engulf me. The knowledge of where we're headed clogs my throat. Sterile rooms. Stern faces. My stomach goes cold.

In the ambulance's side mirror, I catch sight of Tristan limping behind us. The city speeds by like a video projected across his body. But Tristan remains constant, never more than a few feet behind the van.

When we arrive at the hospital, Barstow flashes his badge, and the EMTs escort me into the ER so fast my head spins. After a game of twenty questions, a CAT scan, and an assortment of other tests, I sit on a long, thin mattress covered in plastic while a nurse prepares to draw blood. I'm out of the scratchy hospital gown and back in my tank top and jeans, but the sight of the gleaming needle makes my skin crawl.

She's only trying to help, I remind myself. *Take a deep breath. You're in control, not them.* Sitting on the examination table, I peer around the cramped white room filled with cupboards, trays, and a small metal table, desperately trying not to focus on the row of plastic vials about to be filled with my blood.

Where is Tristan when I need a distraction?

As if on cue, his warm chuckle breaks the silence, and I jolt in surprise. The nurse sends me a withering look.

"Sorry."

Tristan rests coolly against the wall—but his arm is still wound gingerly around his side.

<Quit complaining, Plant Girl. I had my wound stitched up with practically no pain meds. Surely you can handle a few pokes.>

"I'm not a post-apocalyptic macho-man." I suck in a breath as the nurse plunges the needle into my arm, wiggling the tip back and forth toward my vein.

The pricking pain soon fades into a distant memory. My eyelids flutter shut, and I'm in another white-walled room Someone is pressing a needle into my arm—a man wearing a surgical mask. I'm lying down, my eight-year-old body trembling as strange men do painful things to me. I feel the slice of a knife against the back of my head before anesthesia sweeps me into oblivion.

I shoot up in the chair, gasping for air. My eyes rake the clinic.

"Calm down, Miss Johnson. Everything's all right."

The nurse's voice sounds distant. Shudders sweep my chest. My arms shake.

What did those men do to me? Did they perform an operation on my head?

Fingernails dig into my wrists, and I see the nurse's plastic gloves gripping my hands. She says something, but the words are out of reach.

Through blurry vision, I can make out the needle's slender shape pricking my arm—just like the needles those strange men used on me again and again.

I can't breathe.

<Fern, listen to me. You're going to be fine. Focus on my words.> Tristan's strong, familiar voice filters into my frantic mind. Firm. Warm. Reassuring.

Sucking down gulps of air, I rivet my attention on Tristan. The concern in his eyes. Those firm lips. The splash of freckles on his nose. The determined look he always wears when he's trying to help me.

He grips my hand tightly. *<You're here to get help. This nurse is trying to find out what the scientists did to you. There's no danger here. I've got you.>*

I silently repeat those words over and over. *There's no danger here. I've got you.*

I hope with all my heart they're true.

After a few seconds, my heart slows, breathing growing even. Tristan smooths a strand of my copper hair, rubbing it between his fingers. *<How are you feeling?>*

I take a deep breath. "I'm good."

"I'm glad you're all right now." The nurse peers at me, looking right through Tristan. "What happened?"

I flash her a weary smile. "Just a bad memory."

"Well, be sure to tell me if you feel woozy again."

I nod. She checks the vial of blood attached to the needle in my arm. Glancing at the table behind her, I realize she's already filled three other vials.

"Your medical report says you were diagnosed with psychosis."

"Oh, I'm not crazy. I just see into another world."

From the confused expression on her rosy face, I might as well have barked like a dog. Or spoken in Swahili.

I shift on the hard table and notice an agent hovering by the door. "Don't I get one phone call, to a lawyer or something?"

The nurse glances at the agent. When he nods, she ducks out of the room. She returns a few minutes later with a cell phone nestled in the palm of her hand. "Make it fast."

I take the phone, slide gingerly off the table, and dial Elinore's number.

Instead of her soft, high-pitched voice, I hear the woman I'd hired to babysit her.

"Fern, is that you?"

"Yes, Mrs. Kent. I'm calling to check on Elinore."

"I've been trying to get a hold of you all morning.

There was a car accident. On our way to the park."

I suck in a gasp.

"We were T-boned by a truck pulling out of a parking lot. Elinore was closest to the door on that side, so she took the brunt of it. An ambulance rushed her to Saint Matthew's Children's Hospital. She just went into surgery."

I open my mouth, but no words come out. My little girl is hurt so badly she needs surgery, and I'm not even going to be there when she comes out of it.

"W-what's wrong? How bad is it?"

Mrs. Kent hesitates. "Her arm is shattered in several places, her leg broken, and her hip was dislocated. They won't know the full extent of the injuries till they're in surgery. They said you should be prepared for the worst."

I drop to my knees. Tears streak my cheeks. The world spins.

"She's a brave little girl. She didn't even cry much. But she kept asking for you."

The agent taps his watch, his brows arched.

Tristan kneels beside me, one hand on my back. *<Tell her what she needs to know.>*

Pushing through the panic rising in my chest, I force a steadying breath. "Thank you so much for taking care of her, Mrs. Kent. I'll be there as soon as I possibly can."

But right now I have to make a choice between one little girl who means the world to me and a world full of total strangers.

"I'm actually in a hospital myself." Another sob cuts me off. "But the second I'm free, I'll be there. Which hospital are you at?"

"Saint Matthew's. I'll let her know you're on your way."

I thank her again, then hang up. Yearning to redial and promise to be at Elinore's side in minutes, I rise shakily to my feet and give the phone back to the nurse. She passes it to the stiff agent.

"My niece was in a car accident and is having surgery. Can we finish up here soon?"

The nurse's charcoal eyes show concern. "I'm so sorry to hear that. But we need you here a little longer. You have to go a few hours without food or drink in order for the tests to be run properly. I'm truly sorry." She exits the room, taking the agent with her. I have no doubt he'll remain stationed outside my door.

I should be perched next to my little fairy, telling her stories and decorating the room with pink balloons. Instead, I'm getting my body drained of blood to stop an unstoppable monster.

Perfect.

Chapter Nine

After being poked, prodded, scanned, and sliced, I'm sent to a recovery room to wait. For what, I can't guess, but with Tristan slumped on the floor beside my chair, at least I don't have to wonder alone.

But my normally animated friend is unusually quiet. If we can't close the rift and stop the Rhoon, I could lose him today.

I rip my attention from Tristan, searching for something to distract my thoughts. All I find is a cotton wad taped to my inner arm where the needles pricked me. Which reminds me of Elinore and the invasive surgery she must be undergoing right now.

For a second, panic claws at my throat. I should

be with El, but if I leave, Tristan could die.

I'll lose them both.

No. I won't let that happen.

Slowly counting my heartbeats and regulating my breaths, I channel the anxiety into the pressure of my nails burrowing into my palms. Blood trickles down my wrists, sealing the promise.

My heartbeat echoes in my ears, and the room seems to fluctuate in time to its rhythm. The lines of reality blur as dust and a cracked landscape shift into focus. Then, just as suddenly, it's gone.

Tristan stares at me, biting the inside of his cheek. *<You're getting stronger. And the rift is growing wider.>*

I dip a finger into the pool of golden dust on the arm of my chair. The sand clings to my fingertip. It vibrates, stinging a bit.

"Let's just hope those tests reveal something useful."

After several long minutes, the door to the small room creaks open. Agent Barstow enters with two agents on his heels. I wipe away the blood smearing my palms.

As he approaches, a paper envelope under his arm catches my attention. He stands beside my chair, as rigid and foreboding as ever.

With his unwavering eyes fixated on me, I rub at the thin bandages that cover the puncture wounds on my arms. "Did you find something?"

He slips an X-ray out of the cardboard sleeve and places it on the small table between us. I rise out of my chair for a better view. It's an image of someone's head—and my name is imprinted on the top corner.

There's a shuffling sound at the door. A balding doctor steps inside, nodding toward the agents before crossing to stand behind the table.

"I'm Dr. Narcen, a neurologist. I specialize in sensory cases." He traces long, gnarled fingers over the shaded image. "We didn't have sufficient time to properly analyze everything we found in the readings of your cerebral cortex, but what we have been able to conclude is unique."

"Unique?" I've been called many things but never that.

His thin lab coat brushes against the table's edge. "Our brains are constantly absorbing energy so they can work efficiently without forcing the rest of our bodies to digest massive energy sources. The synapses only fire and compute in various portions of our brain at a time."

Tristan stifles a yawn.

The neurologist rubs his curled hands together. "Every region of the human brain is used at some point, but only sixteen percent of it is used at any given time. This is a natural form of energy preservation, allowing us to process information and remain conscious. Your brain, however, seems to be functioning differently."

Tristan steps toward the table, peering at the X-rays, thumb rubbing absently at the dirt caking his armor.

I squelch the urge to scratch an itch beginning to creep along my hairline. "How so?"

"You are firing synapses in as much as twenty-five percent of your brain at a time. The majority of that is in specific sections of the frontal and parietal lobes—the areas used to differentiate thought, dream, and reality. They incorporate the physical senses and tell the rest of the body whether what it's experiencing is real or not."

Barstow's shoes scuff the tiled floor. "What does all that mean for the issue at hand?"

Narcen's full, sterile attention trains on me. "It means Fern was either born with the inability to differentiate between what is physical and what is imaginary..." *Basically the worldwide description for insanity.* "Or someone altered her brain to make it hypersensitive."

Everyone in the room stares at me like I'm some kind of lab rat. Everyone except Tristan, who's wearing that infernal smirk. *<I knew you were special.>*

A guttural noise gurgles in the back of my throat. "So I'm warped. My brain is screwed up."

The neurologist scratches his balding hairline. "Whether or not this came about by choice, your thought processes are able to work through this device." He motions with a bob of his chin for Barstow and me to move closer. Then he jabs a gnarled index finger at the dark picture, identifying a thin white rectangle about three inches from where my spine trails into the cranium.

"Is that some kind of chip?"

"Yes. It's a neuro-kinetic link. How did you know?"

I shrug. "I watch a lot of sci-fi."

The impressed look falls a few notches. "We have no way of knowing what this chip does. However, in light of recent events, our best guess is that it has something to do with your ability to see through space and time."

"That chip is what allows me to see through the rift?"

Barstow straightens so quickly he almost tips the chair over. "There's a scientific reason behind this anomaly?"

He probably didn't mean to sound quite so relieved.

Narcen hesitates, then nods.

I rub a finger at the nape of my neck, feeling a slight scar there—so tiny I'd never given it much thought before. "So I tore a hole in the fabric of space and time because that chip lets me see through the parallels and manipulate the rift?"

Tristan's head snaps up. *<That's what they*

THE GIRL WHO COULD SEE

meant!>

Barstow clears his throat loudly. "Okay, then tell me how to shut it down."

Narcen studies the X-rays again. "We would need more time to properly examine—"

"We don't have time," Barstow snaps, fist slamming down on the table. "That hole is widening, and a planet-destroying monster is ready to come through." His words trail off, and he shakes his head. "I can't believe I just said that out loud."

Tristan scans the room, foot tapping the floor, and I can almost see the wheels turning in his head. Crossing back to me, he grabs my hand. *<I need to go check on something. Don't let them do anything until I get back, okay?>*

My head spins so fast all I can manage is a quick nod. He disappears like a cool breath of wind.

Barstow's knuckles pale as he grips the back of the chair he's standing behind. "I can tell from the look on your face that the invisible boy is talking to you. What did he say?"

"He said he needed to go check on something, and we shouldn't do anything till he gets back."

The broad-shouldered agent rolls his eyes. "If only we had the leisure to wait around for your imaginary friend to make time for the end of the world. But we don't. If he tells you anything important, let me know immediately. In the meantime, we need to find this rift thing and figure out how to shut it down. Doctor?"

Narcen shifts his weight from one foot to the other. "Theoretically, if we remove the chip from Miss Johnson's head, we should be able to shut down her link to the rift and close the breach. The best neurologists in the state are working as we speak to find a way to remove that chip with minimal brain damage."

Minimal brain damage? How generous.

"Are you kidding? How about we go for *no* brain damage." I turn my stare from the doctor to the agent. "Besides, you don't seriously believe that's how I can see through the rift, do you? A computer chip in my head?"

The doctor's shaking hands weave circles in the air as he talks emphatically. "It would take us months, years even, to fully understand how the technology works. However, from what we have determined, it seems clear that the chip altering your frontal lobe allows you to see things we never even imagined were possible."

I collapse into the chair behind me. "That doesn't explain how Tristan can see me. I don't think he has a chip in his head. And when I held his hand, Barstow saw Tristan too."

The doctor scrubbed at his chin. "My best guess is that you are linked to the rift through that chip. Because of this, you were able to tear it open, expand it, and allow others to see what you see—if the rift is open wide enough. Somehow, you are also linked to the young man you've been seeing in the same way as you are linked to his world. By opening the rift wider, you can strengthen that link, holding him steady in this world just enough for others to see him."

I feel like I'm missing a vital piece of the puzzle. "So, if I opened the rift—then I'm the reason the Rhoon is able to get through?"

Narcen's mouth pulls into a tight line. "In a way, yes. Although the rift is widening at a rate beyond your control, you are able to speed up the process.

Once we extract the chip, however, your link will be permanently extinguished, and the rift should close."

Barstow's arms tighten over his chest. "More importantly—we can use that device in your head to find the rift and clear the area of any possible casualties." He glances over his shoulder at the two men in suits hovering behind him. "Get our best technicians working on this. You already have the readings from the tests she did. Tell them we need a location in under an hour." His thick fingers tap against the wall.

"What about me?"

"You're staying right here. We can't afford to have civilians getting in the way of an FBI operation."

"No way," I grind out, bolting out of my chair to stand rigidly. "Tristan said we couldn't do anything till he gets back. Besides, you wouldn't have known about this without me! I'm only staying here because you said I could help you save lives. Otherwise I would be at the hospital with my niece."

"I can send someone to check on your niece if you'd like. But you're staying here. If Tristan reports any consequential information, tell one of the agents, and they'll relay it to me."

"That's not what—"

"Your country thanks you for helping us identify a threat to national security and countless lives. However…" He straightens, towering over me. "This is where your involvement ends."

He leaves the room, bookended by the doctor and his agents. The door slams shut just as I reach it. The *click* of a lock reverberates through the closed door.

I'm trapped again, while others storm off to decide my fate.

Chapter Ten

"Hey!" I wrap my fists around the doorknob and shake it hard. "You can't lock me in here. I need to go see my niece!"

Treading lines into the coarse carpet as I pace, I've screamed myself hoarse, with no response. I've been trapped in this waiting room for a good hour, and Barstow has probably already found the rift's location. Elinore could be out of surgery. And I'm stuck here, waiting for a group of doctors to open up my head.

So not how I thought this day would go.

My frustration morphs into worry. "Tristan, where are you? They said they're going to operate on my brain."

I sink into a chair before the shaking can overtake my legs. When I was younger, shaking legs often turned to wracking shudders—a form of post-traumatic stress, a doctor once said. Hoping to avoid that, I wrap my arms around my chest and focus on my breathing.

<They're planning to do what?>

I jerk my chin up to find Tristan walking toward me, holding a stack of papers. His limp is deeper than I remember, his breathing ragged.

"What happened to you?"

<Took me longer to get back than I expected. I think the rift is expanding—it's getting harder to see into your side. But what's this about brain surgery?>

I gulp down the thickness in my throat. "The doctor said he wants to take out the chip in my head. To cut the link that's widening the rift. It makes sense, but—"

<He can't do that. The chip can only be shut off manually. Extracting it by force will kill you.>

It feels like the weight of the entire hospital is pressing in on my chest. "What?"

<And if they pull it out, they'll open the rift so far the Rhoon can destroy this world in minutes.>

"How do you know all this?"

<I went to the research center...or where it used to be. Some of the files were still intact.> Tristan crouches in front of my chair and hands me the papers.

<When the Rhoon started filtering into my world as the plague, the scientists in our leading cities began searching for a cure. When they realized I was immune, I became their main test subject. They never discovered a cure, but they did find a way to close the rift.>

I run my fingertips over the dog-eared pages. "How?"

He slides back on his haunches to sit beside me, and his eyes search mine.

<Do you remember the first time we met?>

I rack my brain. "I don't think so."

<You were in the lab, strapped to a table.>

An image floats to the surface. A younger me, strapped to an operating table in a pristine white room, with a bandage around my head and terror in my heart. "That must have been just after they implanted the chip. I was so scared. Until you showed up."

Tears prick at my eyes. "You asked if I was okay. When I started crying, you told me everything would be fine. That you'd help me. And you did."

Tristan nudges my shoulder. *<That was the moment when you imprinted on me and our link formed. I became your connection to my world. That connection—our friendship—is what kept me from being poisoned by the Rhoon. Like you, I'm not fully in this world. Our link allows me to see into your world and to be suspended somewhere between it and mine. I can't control the rift the way you can, but I can see through it because of you.>* He paused. *<Following me so far?>*

"Yeah, I think so."

<When that chip in your head allowed you to open the rift, you basically opened a door. A door between our worlds. One that you could close, but I couldn't. When the rift tore through your world and mine, it made us both susceptible to the Rhoon's entrance.>

My brain's beginning to hurt.

<You were there, the first time the Rhoon arrived.>

That memory is less clear. Just fragments of death and dust and pain. "It frightened me."

<Right. So you closed the door on your side. But we were unable to close it on ours, which made my world an easy target for the Rhoon.>

The papers crunch in my fists as the weight of what this means dawns on me. "The chip in my head is the reason the Rhoon could even get to your planet. I killed an entire civilization." I start shaking again, and even Tristan's warm hands covering mine can't slow the shudders.

<It's not your fault. You didn't know what you were doing—>

Wrenching my hands from his grasp, I jerk to my feet. "If we don't get to Barstow soon and tell him how to shut down the rift, I'm going to have the destruction of two planets on my conscience." Although if that happens, I'll be too dead to care.

He looks up at me, an eyebrow arched, as I step around him and stride toward the door, then grab the knob and shake it with all my strength. Nothing.

Releasing a groan, I let go of the handle, step back, and ram a foot into the bottom of the door…which proves far less satisfying than I'd hoped.

"I need to talk to Barstow!" I shout through the tiny window to the pair of guards posted outside. "I have important information for him."

They don't even flinch.

Tristan is back on his feet, standing at my shoulder. *<Fern, calm down. I haven't finished explaining what my people learned about shutting down the rift.>*

His words still my rampage. "What did you find out?"

<You're able to control the rift. And since I'm your link to this world, together we can close the tear.>

I almost laugh out loud. A week ago, I was worried about paying my rent. Now I'm strategizing how to close a tear in the fabric of space and time.

"We can close it by doing what, exactly?"

Tristan breaks eye contact, fidgeting with the strap of his pack for a minute. Just as his lips part, the *click* of a turning lock interrupts his answer. The doorknob rotates, and the door swings open. Dr. Narcen stands in the entryway, flocked by nurses.

"I received the go-ahead from the director of the FBI. We're ready to take you to prep for the operation. Please follow me." Narcen's voice is calm, like he's not about to whisk me away to my death.

"I need to talk to Agent Barstow. Now."

One of the FBI agents stationed in front of my door steps forward. "Barstow is at the location of the rift. Anything he needs to know, you can tell me."

I take a deep breath. *Gotta make this good.* "Tristan discovered that the only way to close the rift is for me to shut it down manually. Taking the chip out of my head will kill me. Which means I won't be able to accomplish the task."

The doctor quizzes me on the details of Tristan's information. I tell him what I know in terms I hope he'll understand.

His forehead puckers. "There is no guarantee that you will be able to close the rift by sheer willpower. I still think extracting the chip is our best option."

You have got *to be kidding me.* "Can we at least talk to Barstow first?"

The doctor motions toward a nurse holding a syringe. "If you do not comply peacefully, we are authorized to use force."

I take a step backward, searching for Tristan. One of the FBI agents grabs my arm, his grip like an iron vice. The nurse comes closer, her syringe pointed at my bicep.

"Tristan!" Cold, stinging reality washes over me as I realize one prick of that needle and I'm dead. Along with the rest of this world. *No, no this isn't happening.* Panic. Filling my throat, drowning me. "Tristan *help!*"

Tristan appears inches away, face drained of color. *<I can't touch them. You need to strengthen our bond.>*

"I-I'm trying."

My chest heaves. I can hardly think anymore, let alone focus on our bond.

<Fern.> Tristan's firm voice freezes my struggling limbs. *<You're in control of reality. You can manipulate it. You don't have to be here.>* He motions to the FBI agent, still holding me in a death grip, and the nurse, syringe poised above my shoulder. Both are staring at me oddly, eyes darting between me and Narcen, waiting for his command. *<You are tied*

to the rift so deeply, it is affected by your emotions.> Tristan's words push back the fog clouding my thoughts.

My entire life I've just tried to survive. To sustain a sense of normalcy. I've never looked beyond the immediate. I've only ever seen my world as the only real one.

Now all I have is the impossible. And faith in an invisible world. And a hope that if I jump, Tristan will be there to catch me.

I close my eyes and reach out to Tristan's world. It wraps around me, invading the room. Embracing it, I let the warm air engulf my body until I feel the dust peppering my face.

<You don't have to play by their rules, so don't let them do this.>

I won't.

I open my eyes just as the nurse shoves the needle into my arm. It passes through me, as if my skin isn't even there.

At that moment, it's not.

The nurse jerks back, glancing frantically around—but not once looking directly at me. I slip out of her grasp and step past the equally confused agent. No one tries to stop me. Heart beating precariously in my throat, I stride across the room—past the doctor and the FBI agents with their shocked expressions— through the doorway.

Tristan's words echo in my head: *you don't have to be here.*

The carpet fades into a desert of sand. The walls grow craggy and bleached. As I step into the hall, the crowd of nurses scurries into the room behind me— walking right through me. As if I'm nothing more than vapor.

My hands tremble, but every step feels surreal. Walking in a dream. Down the hall, I face the outside wall of the hospital. The building continues to fluctuate—I'm not fully in my world or Tristan's, but somewhere in between.

This must be what it feels like for him.

I reach out a hand toward the wall, and it slips right through. I take another step. Instead of slamming into a surface of rough wood, I feel nothing more than a slight vibration. Then the plush grass beneath my shoes dissipates like the sand.

I'm standing outside the hospital on the sprawling lawn edging the road, Tristan beside me.

"That actually worked!" And it was incredible. No wonder Tristan loves making dramatic exits.

As the connection to his world wanes, my body grows tired, heavy. My strength is sapped as I tread the fine line between two worlds.

The alien landscape fades away, leaving only Tristan and a flicker of dust glinting in the sunlight. I can't hold back a laugh. "What just happened?"

<The deeper you step into my world, the more yours fades away, to the point that it cannot physically touch you.>

"That's pretty cool."

<Yeah, it is. Unless you actually want *to be in that other world.>* He stares at me, lips parted, then shakes his head. *<What now?>*

"I'm not sure." Scanning the road and parking lot, I search for Barstow's vehicle. "We have no way of knowing where Barstow is. Or the rift, for that matter. And there's a little girl who's waited far too long for some company."

I wave down a taxi. When the driver pulls over, I

slide into the backseat.

"Where you headed?"

I give him the address to the children's hospital.

To find a little girl and hopefully save the world.

Chapter Eleven

The route through Los Angeles is familiar. I've ridden a bus down long sections of it every day to my job on Hollywood Boulevard. Still, as I watch out the window of the taxi, it's hard to tell the difference between LA and Tristan's apocalyptic world. Where there should be sidewalks full of people or towering buildings, all I see are decaying constructions that are little more than dangerous wreckage.

There's a soft rustle next to me as Tristan runs his hands over the textured seat. I suggested he try riding along, and he's become enamored with the slick feel of the leather. As his world becomes clearer to me, apparently mine—at least the scenery that's closest to me—is also growing more tangible for him. It's enough to add fresh color to his cheeks.

There's a strain on my body as I hold the car in place around him. Not that I'm about to tell Tristan that.

"What are those?" I ask, pointing at a small cluster of round-roofed hovels so pale they look like ghosts resting in a desert.

<That's where the singles live. Once you reach thirteen years, you get kicked out of your home to live in a dome like that until you find the person you want to spend the rest of your life with. It's pretty much a constant party. Or it was. Before...you know.>

I gulp. *Before I destroyed his planet, including his friends and family. And maybe...someone who was more? Had he found the woman he wanted to spend his life with?*

The question burns like a coal in my throat, but I don't dare ask it. Maybe I don't want to know the answer.

"So, where do you live now?"

<My bunker.> He leans back in the chair, sighing against the smooth leather of the seatback. *<An old*

storm shelter that I've reinforced. It's pretty spacious since it's just me, and I've been able to save some food there out of reach of the Rhoon.>

"You'll have to try some of our food once all this is finished."

<I have been dying to have one of those hot dog things.>

I can only shake my head, returning to look out the window.

When the taxi driver turns down West Temple Street, alarm bells scream in my mind. Sweat dots my forehead. Snatches of memory come quickly—like flashes of lightning illuminating a room for only a second.

In my mind, I see worn asphalt cascading beneath my bare feet. *But when did this happen?* Chain-link fences pressing into my palms. *But why?*

The reason seems so close, but every time I nearly grasp hold, it slips away with a burning sensation...a subconscious warning that I'd buried these memories long ago on purpose. I clench quaking fists and glance at Tristan.

His face is ashen. *<You'll have to remember*

eventually. It's the only way.>

"For now, can we just focus on finding Elinore?"

With a shrug, Tristan reaches through the car seat and pumps his legs in a half jog. Part of his body hovers inside the taxi; the rest disappears beneath the floor. *<My side is solidifying again, which means we must be getting close to the rift. We'll meet up after you park.>*

With that, he drops from sight.

I stare through the smudged windshield as Saint Matthew's Children's Hospital rises into view. Behind it, some kind of construction site is cornered by yellow-and-black hazard tape.

I'm coming, El.

But just as we start to turn down the road leading to the hospital, I spot two cop cars and a stoic FBI agent. They seem to be re-routing traffic—while a lot of it is streaming from the hospital and onto the main road. *I thought people hurry to the hospital, not away?*

"I don't think you'll be getting in today, ma'am," the taxi driver tells me over his shoulder.

I lean forward, trying to catch his eyes in the rearview mirror. "I have to try. Drive up closer to that cop and the FBI agent—I need to talk to him."

A bead of sweat spots the driver's forehead, but he does as I say, driving around the other cars making U-turns and up to the agent and policewoman. As the taxi driver rolls down both our windows, I get a better look at the agent standing beside the brunette woman. His intense emerald eyes and slicked-back dark hair are hard to forget. This is the agent who was posted outside my FBI interrogation.

He must recognize me, too, because while the woman continues to wear a slightly confused expression as she explains to my driver that we have to turn around—no one is allowed beyond this point— the agent's smooth features crinkle into a frown.

"What are you doing here?"

It's directed at me, and he steps closer to the taxi.

"I need to talk to Barstow. Please. It's vitally important."

The agent stares at me for a stretching moment, then he tips his head, no longer staring, just watching. Taking me in. Deciding whether I'm trustworthy.

He must decide that I am, because he steps back to speak to the policewoman. After a few seconds, they both wave us closer, rather than turning us around like the other cars.

"All right, impossible girl. Go tell Barstow how to stop another catastrophe."

Gratitude lifts my heart like a pair of wings. "But, why…?"

He lifts one shoulder in a half shrug, "Because if we'd believed you sooner, maybe none of this would have escalated."

The weight of the responsibility those words carry is not lost on me, but only affirms my resolve. I couldn't stop the Rhoon from destroying that building a week ago—but this time I have the chance to actually do something about it. I can't let that opportunity slip by.

As we enter the parking lot, sleek black vans surround the hospital, and yellow tape and thick orange cones block off a wide perimeter. A fire truck has even made an appearance, while the unfortunately familiar presence of FBI agents in bulletproof vests fills the parking lot.

Why are they here?

But the FBI are not the only ones crowding

around the hospital. Police officers and nurses whisk children in wheelchairs and rolling beds from the towering white building. I spot some civilians—who must be parents—following the children as they're settled into ambulances and other vehicles. Within minutes, said vehicles are full and pulling out of the lot to join the funnel of automobiles trying to get onto the main road.

It's an evacuation. The hospital is being evacuated.

My taxi pulls into a parking spot, and the engine's steady hum dies as the door unlocks with a hitch. But my limbs won't budge. My thoughts swirl. Splinters of distant memories flit through my brain so quickly I can hardly keep up.

A deep gash in my leg. My parents taking me to the closest hospital. Days spent on a scratchy cot surrounded by nurses and needles.

Doctors with gravelly voices and strange requests. A large tube scanning my whole body. Shocked expressions. Then, darkness. Being so tired that numbness and sleep are welcome.

But what came after was definitely not.

My head throbs, refusing to let me delve any deeper into the past. Part of me is thankful. I don't want to know what happened next.

"Miss Johnson? There's an FBI agent walking toward us. Are you in some kind of trouble?"

I focus and catch sight of Barstow stalking across the crowded parking lot. Even the police officers step aside for him.

After stumbling out the door, I pay the driver, assuring him that I'm not doing anything illegal. As the taxi pulls out, I look past Barstow's rigid figure at the structure behind him. The towering white building glares down at me as the frantic figures streaming from its doors fill the air with tension.

Agent Barstow's scowl rivets on me. "How did you find us?"

He's wearing a bulletproof vest too. The holster strapped to his side reveals a pistol beneath his large coat.

"I came for Elinore."

His eyes narrow. "How did you get out of the hospital room?"

"Long story. But here's what you need to know:

Tristan says I'm the only one who can shut down the rift, but they can't remove the chip from my head— that'll kill me." I try to push aside my desperation to find Elinore long enough to explain what's needed. "Someone from each side has to manually cut off the link. Which means you need me. And Tristan."

He eyes me for a second, then barks orders into a microphone attached to his earpiece, telling the agents with Dr. Narcen to stand down. "You'd better not make me regret this."

"You believe me?"

He groans. "Don't sound so surprised. Nothing about this case has been normal, but the only people who seem to know anything about it are you and that boy. If Tristan says he knows how to stop it, I'm far more likely to believe him than a bunch of doctors doing guesswork."

A smile begins at the edge of my mouth. "I agree, sir." Scanning the area again, I chew on my lip. "What's all this?"

"A perimeter. We've tried to prepare for the threat the best we can, starting with an immediate evacuation of the hospital and surrounding area—but it's painstakingly slow."

He practically groans on that last word.

"Have you been able to find the rift's location, then? It's the hospital?"

"We've traced the same frequency here as the one that chip in your head was giving off. Not to mention the radioactive decay that's soaking this area. And then there's *that*." His thumb jerks over his shoulder toward the mountain of rubble in the distance.

"What is that?" It's definitely not a construction site like I'd assumed before.

"The first building the Rhoon took down. The one you told us about."

I gulp. *Imagine what it would do to this whole city...* "We'd better find that rift fast."

And El even faster.

His arms fold tightly across his chest, denting the padded vest. "We have dozens of men searching the building, but we haven't been able to find the source of the rift. Or the creature that destroyed that building. I'm not even sure I should let a civilian step foot in there..."

He won't let me stay unless I can convince him he

needs me. My gaze filters over his shoulder. The yellow hazard tape that keeps people out but locks me in. Nurses and children flowing from the building in a constant stream of panic. Uniformed police officers and rigid FBI agents—a stark contrast to the flood of white coats and gowns. The evacuation has probably been underway for some time, and despite how much I strain my eyes looking for her, El is nowhere to be found in the throng of bodies.

I can only hope she's already been taken home...until I spot a tan minivan parked a few rows of parking spaces away and catch my breath. It belongs to Mrs. Kent.

Elinore is still here—and the FBI may not even let me inside to see her, let alone shut down the rift.

My hands curl into fists, nails leaving crescent imprints on my palms. I need to know Elinore is okay. But I have to convince Barstow to let me stay first.

Tristan appears at my shoulder. *<I could probably find it faster from my side, but you'll have to translate where it is on yours.>*

I grab Barstow's arm. "I'll help with anything you need and not get in your way. I just need to know where you've searched. Please, let me stay."

The FBI agent rakes a sharp gaze over me. But he agrees to let me stay. He ushers me—and inadvertently, Tristan—inside the hospital, along with a group of agents following his every move.

We weave through people swarming out of the building as if it were on fire. When I step through the double doors, Barstow's men, heavily armed and clad in bulletproof vests, cluster around me, shielding me from the thick outpour of bodies.

More agents are inside, guiding the wave of nurses heading for the door. But the local police force has the evacuation mostly under control—or as under control as a building full of fearful people dashing for the door can be.

Medical assistants steer children toward the exit. A little redheaded boy hunches in a wheelchair. A girl hobbles along on crutches as her nurse carries an IV dripping fluid into her arm. The flood of kids and white-coated adults swirls around me.

"Please move quickly and efficiently, without endangering those around you," a deep voice echoes through the hospital's speaker system. "Nurses, if any children are in need of assistance, ask a police officer for help."

The message plays on repeat, mingling with the wails and uproar of voices.

I freeze in the midst of the flood, tempted to make my way to the chairs against the wall where parents are peppering nurses with questions regarding their children's whereabouts, and see if Mrs. Kent is there. But a curving reception desk directly ahead, cluttered with paperwork and tissue boxes, catches my eye.

"Elinore is here," I whisper to Tristan. "I've got to find her."

His knuckles brush against my elbow, answer enough. I drift toward the reception desk. Barstow tosses me a cautionary glance, and I smile reassuringly.

"I'm looking for a patient. Elinore Sommers?"

The woman's hair sticks out at odd angles, and she doesn't even bother to look up from her computer. "Room number?"

"I'm not sure. She was having surgery after a car accident."

The woman's thin fingers fly across the keyboard,

but I'm not certain if they're hastening to my aid. The seconds tick by until she finally glances up. "There's no record of an Elinore Sommers having been admitted here."

Tristan's fist slams into the counter. I gape at her. "But I was told just a few hours ago that she was taken here. Try Martha Kent. That's the woman who brought her."

The nurse turns back to her computer screen. "Not that I can see."

I stumble backward. A flash of white lab coat jostles my unsteady steps. I bump into another FBI agent standing against the wall.

"My...my niece." I try to explain, but his expression is aloof. I jerk away from him just in time to see Barstow retreating down the hall. He's surrounded by other agents, all sliding as effortlessly as bullets through the crowd.

I take off after him. Elbowing through the frantic crowd, I pass a small blond boy—about Elinore's age—with a smattering of freckles, sitting in a wheelchair, his arm bandaged. A nurse stands beside him as he waits in a corner of the room. The little boy flops back in his chair with an exaggerated groan, then picks at the paint peeling off the wall beside him with his free hand.

His obvious ease—even boredom—in spite of the evacuation settles my heart's pace a bit. *She'll be okay. You'll find her, and she'll be all right.*

I aim for the hall, pushing at the back of a police officer in my way. The intermingling of voices and the terse tones of the police trying to guide everyone safely toward the exit grates on my already-frayed nerves. Pulse pounding, I shoulder between a nurse and cop deep in conversation and cut around a girl limping on a crutch. Barstow is only feet away now—

Tristan dodges in front of me. <*What are you doing?*>

"I know they brought Elinore here, but that nurse says they have no record of her. It's like she…disappeared."

A chill snakes through my body. *No. She's fine— she has to be. This is not happening again.*

But Tristan's solemn expression tells me it is.

Chapter Twelve

I scan the crowded hospital foyer, eyes lighting on the little boy in the wheelchair who's now poking any nurse who gets too close. Surely Elinore must be waiting around a corner.

What if she's not?

I try to be rational. Why would they—the doctors who took me—care about my niece?

The answer crashes into my chest with enough force to push me back a step. Because she's *my* niece. She shares my DNA.

They'd wanted me for my ability to see Tristan's world. For my mind that could somehow withstand the chip they'd implanted, and even use it to see the impossible. They assume it's hereditary. But it's not. I've told El about Tristan, but never once has she been able to see him.

Fear clamps around my throat with iron-cold fingers. There's no telling what they'll do to her to get the response they want.

Knees buckling, I let the sway of the crowd push me toward the side of the room. I press my palm against the wall, feeling cool, textured paint beneath my skin. The sensation roots me here, dragging me from the shadows of my mind.

<You have to talk to Agent Barstow.>

"I've already told him everything."

<You haven't told him the details of your kidnapping. Your imprisonment. What those doctors did to you here.>

I don't want to remember those things. "I'm not even sure it was here—"

Pain explodes in my skull, and I reach for Tristan's shoulder, grappling with the padded armor encasing it. The headache brings another stream of memories.

I'm lying on a silver table, arms and legs cinched

down. Needles prick my joints as a doctor leans over me, a white mask covering his face. A scalpel hovers in his gloved hand.

I scream, severing the memory. My knees give out, and I fall to the tile floor. Slick material brushes my face. The sound of footsteps echoes around me, along with the creak of wheels sliding past. I'm safe, I know, but my body still shakes like it did that day on the table. I can't get the tremors to stop.

<*Take a deep breath. It's all right. Let the memories in.*>

Warm hands wrap around my waist as Tristan gently pulls me closer and presses his chin to the top of my head. Ignoring the blood thundering in my veins, I concentrate on his even breathing—a sensation I'm still not used to.

After a few minutes, I rise to my feet, shaky but alert. Most of the police in the crowded waiting room are still moving, guiding patients and parents outside. But the crowd has started to thin.

Peering over Tristan's shoulder, I see the little blond boy in the wheelchair. He lifts a hand to wave, lips parting to reveal a gap-toothed smile that lights up his pale face. Elinore smiles like that, and the memory lights a spark of hope in my chest.

I flash a wave at the little boy.

If I don't talk to Barstow, Elinore may suffer the same fate I did. Or worse. But I refuse to let that happen. When I disappeared, no one came looking. This time, I'll move heaven and earth to see that smile again.

Tristan and I march down the hallway, speckled with numbered doors and posters of smiling children—quite a contrast to the fearful expressions on the young patients being rushed to the front door. For several minutes, white coats, wheelchairs, and frightened faces block my view. When I catch sight of Barstow, he is speaking with a woman in her late twenties who's waving her hands frantically.

A woman I know.

"Mrs. Kent!" I race forward as they both turn to look at me.

"You know her?" Barstow's silvery brows rise.

I grab the woman's shoulders. "Where's El?"

Her lips quiver. Thin scratches and a black eye mar her pale complexion. A detached part of my mind realizes she must have been injured in the car accident that brought Elinore here.

"They said they were taking her in for surgery." Her wild eyes dart around. "But she never came out. I waited in the recovery room for hours. When I finally asked when she'd be done…" Her fingers wind through greasy brown hair. "They said they didn't know who I was talking about. That they didn't have a little girl who'd been in a car crash."

An icy chill sweeps over me. *I'd really like to wake up from this nightmare now.*

Her mouth emits a sound somewhere between a hiccup and a sob. "I can't find her anywhere, Fern!"

I lay a shaking hand on her shoulder, then glance at Agent Barstow. His scowl deepens.

Tristan's lips twist into a calculating grimace. *<Ask if they did a CAT scan on Elinore.>*

When I repeat the question to Mrs. Kent, she nods slowly. "They said they wanted to be sure there was no brain damage."

Tristan slips one of his flails from the pack at his back, squeezing the handle so tightly I fear he'll split the wood.

I assure Mrs. Kent that she doesn't need to wait here any longer, and she practically runs from the hospital.

Barstow tugs on his collar. "I hope your friend can give me a better explanation than another missing-persons case. I've had enough nightmares for one day."

Amen to that.

Tristan's hands circle tighter around the leather-wrapped handle. *<If Elinore was taken by the same people who experimented on you, Barstow's agents have been looking in the wrong place.>*

When I relay this to Barstow, he curses under his breath. "Where does he think the rift is?"

I know what Tristan's answer will be even before he opens his mouth. *<Under us.>*

"We've checked the hospital blueprints—there's nothing below this floor."

"I think there's some sort of illegal laboratory beneath the building."

His gaze pierces me. "And why would you think that?"

I flinch, not wanting to relive the memories I've

tried so hard to forget. "I was kept down there for three years."

Barstow rakes fingers through his graying hair. "That would explain some things. Why didn't you tell me this before?"

Tristan's nod encourages me to keep going. "I hadn't put it all together myself. Those years were like hell. I blocked the memories and tried to live a normal life."

Barstow's attention shifts to the white earpiece trailing over the back of his ear. He listens, nods, then looks back at me. "So how does all of *this* fit into the end of the world?"

My hands sink into the pockets of my jeans. "I think those experiments may have caused the rift."

Because of me, Tristan lost everything. Because of me, there's a monster threatening Los Angeles. Because of me, Elinore is held captive by the very scientists who stole my childhood.

I'm losing everything...

The weight of it threatens to crush what little hope I have left.

Tristan steps in front of me, and his thumb slips

beneath my chin, lifting my gaze to meet his. *<We'll find Elinore. I promise—we'll make this right. In the meantime, you're going to have to remember how to get to the lab.>*

Drawing in a long breath, I force down the anxiety stabbing at my chest. My pulse quickens. *It's not over yet.* "I thought you were going to lead us, Tristan. After all, you found me there years ago, when I was really young. You probably remember better than I do."

<I might be able to find the cell again from my world.> He wraps the flail's chain around its wooden handle, then stows the weapon in his pack. *<But there's no way I could lead you and those agents through this hospital since I can't see much around you. My connection to the rift isn't as strong as yours.>*

Disappointment settles over me like a dark cloud, but I give him a stiff nod.

Barstow barks orders into his earpiece. "Agents Harley and Ives, I want all pedestrians at least three miles away from this building. The rest of you, convene at the central hallway on the first floor."

His brooding stare locks on me. "While the police and nurses evacuate the premises, you'll guide my agents and me down to this secret level." A muscle ticks in his jaw. "But you don't so much as wave your hand unless I give the order."

I give him the most convincing smile I can muster, fully intending to throw caution to the wind if that's what it takes to save Elinore. "Yes, sir."

Barstow marches down the hall, then turns a corner that leads us into a deserted wing of the hospital—a sharp contrast to the brimming entryway and hall we'd left. While Barstow briefs the agents who spill into the wing from all sides, I step away and tuck myself into an empty corner. Rubbing my numb hands together to spark some feeling in them, I try to calm the tornado whirling in my mind. My eyes slip closed, and I reach into the far recesses of my memory. My thoughts skitter throughout the hospital, searching for the entrance I once used.

But every time I draw close to that ominous door, a little girl's scream reverberates through my head, jarring my concentration.

It's Elinore.

I know the sound isn't real, but the danger is. Those monsters have her. Below my feet. Hidden in a windowless prison that was my world for years. And if they're doing to her half the things they did to me...

"I can't do this."

Chapter Thirteen

It's even less than a whisper, but Tristan hears it. His warm fingertips brush my closed lids. *<You're not the same girl you were then, Fern. You are so much stronger.>*

I want to whimper that he's wrong, but even my voice feels frail.

<Those men tried to take away your ability to live. Even after you escaped. Your shrink, the people at your school, your family...everyone has been telling you you're broken and can't be fixed.>

I hold my breath, not wanting the words to ring as true as they do. *<But they're wrong.>*

He pauses, letting those three words wash over me, fill my mind, and chase away the screams.

<What makes you different makes you exceptional, Fern.>

I open my eyes to see him towering over me. Smudges of blood leak from the bandage at his side, and his tan skin is crisscrossed with silver scars. He's totally out of place here. And dangerous. But I trust this man more than anyone I've ever known.

"If I'm not broken, then what am I?"

Tristan's voice softens. *<You're the only one on this planet who is truly whole.>* His palms descend on my shoulders as he leans forward, filling my view. *<Show others how to see like you do. Starting with those men below us.>*

His words hang in the air as his eyes rivet on mine.

"You know, you could make good money as a motivational speaker."

He chuckles. *<I may have to try that after we save the world.>*

I slip my hand into his. And the crippling fear I've fought my entire life no longer holds me captive. Then

I remember.

"Tristan, grab a keycard from one of the important-looking staff."

<You got it.> He steps through the nearest wall, vanishing from sight.

Barstow finds me in the corner. "You ready?"

"Yes." More than ready.

With a legion of FBI agents following stiffly in my wake, I move quickly down a series of hallways. We pass bed wards and a room marked *Radiology*. As we turn another corner, I feel Tristan's hand slip something into mine. The keycard.

I stop beside a door that has a thick metal box with a slot in the top. I slide the card through the scanner, and the massive door unlocks. I push it inward to reveal rows upon rows of shelving, holding a varied assortment of medications.

"This doesn't look like an entrance to me," Agent Barstow murmurs.

Ignoring the pessimistic agent, I stride past the racks toward an adjoining room. The plaque on the door reads *Blood Bank Supply*. The security system consists of a keypad, scanner, and thumbprint pad—

suspiciously over-secure for a blood bank.

I spin back toward Barstow. "I don't think I can get into this room."

Barstow's hand goes to his holster. "Step away."

I move back down the hall with the rest of the agents. Barstow raises his firearm, and three quick shots ring through the air. The explosions are abrupt but controlled, tearing a hole in the side of the locking mechanism, shattering the scanner and thumbprint pad. Wafting a hand through the air to disperse the residual smoke, Barstow steps forward and lands a heavy kick on the door. It groans in protest but eventually swings away.

Elinore's distant screams—or are they mine?— ricochet in my head as I peek around the door. The empty chamber's floor has a large, rectangular opening in the middle. As my feet carry me closer, I realize the nearest edge of the gap slopes downward into a long ramp, descending beyond my vision. A row of iridescent bulbs set into the wall follow the ramp into thick darkness, their dull light only managing to create pools of shadows.

An image flickers in my mind—a girl strapped to

a long table and wheeled down that ramp toward a room that would become the end of her childhood.

"This is it." The words barely make it out of my constricted throat.

Barstow rubs a hand across his stubbled jaw, shaking his dark head at the sloping entrance. "Maybe you're not so crazy after all." He motions for me to get behind him. I stand right behind his broad shoulders. Other agents form lines to box me in. Their presence should make me feel safer—their muscular bodies, the clicking of their handguns—but I suddenly have a hard time breathing.

I search for Tristan and spot his bobbing shoulders behind me, just beyond the mass of agents. Before I can call out to him, Barstow starts moving downward, following the ramp. I'm swept along. Each step is a dull thud in the suffocating silence, bringing me closer to the one place I swore to never return.

You're doing this for Elinore, Fern. Hold it together.

My eyes rake the area around me, searching for reassurance. The FBI agents all wear the same resolute, emotionless expression. In the midst of their nearly identical, stiff forms, something shimmers in the dim light. Something sharp and vicious.

The spiked balls dangling from the handles in Tristan's tight grip catch the light menacingly. I pity the man—or creature—that tries to face him.

I take the next step with renewed certainty. The first time I came to this place, I was a prisoner. A helpless child. This time, I'm going to make those doctors with their harsh, probing hands feel helpless.

Our footsteps echo through the sloping tunnel like a steady heartbeat as we match our pace to Barstow's. A gangly agent at the front of the group fiddles with an odd device in his hands, and I notice Barstow watching the man out of the corner of his eye.

"What's that?" I lean forward to tap the younger agent's shoulder.

"What? Oh—this. It's a Geiger counter. Measures radiation. It's also helping pinpoint the location of the rift. It traces the degree of radioactive decay as the area surrounding the rift breaks down at the molecular level."

I blink. "That sounds…pleasant. By the way, my name is—"

"Fern Johnson. I know who you are."

I quirk an eyebrow at him. He shrugs. "News spreads fast, especially when it's about a girl who can see through worlds. I'm Jared Maxoe."

"Nice to meet you."

I study the square, yellow box that he holds in one hand. Trailing from the box is a thin wand that must be taking the readings. I watch the numbers flitting across the screen climb for a moment before I step back so Maxoe can continue undistracted.

As we go deeper underground, I sense what feels like the vibrations of a mild earthquake. It must be a side effect of Tristan's world fluctuating around me. But with each step, the vibrations grow stronger.

As I study the sloping ramp, it fades into a deep, sand-covered basin. And the parallel scenery doesn't seem to be experiencing an earthquake. In fact, the collapsed buildings and rotting landscape look almost peaceful.

Drifting toward the edge of the group of agents, I peer around for a familiar blond warrior. "Tristan, what is that?"

He speeds up to join me, his feet sinking into the

dust as he plods beside me. *<I don't know. It's getting more difficult for me to see anything on your side.>*

"Did you feel those tremors?" I keep my voice low but still garner odd looks from the agents clustered around me.

<No.>

The ground shakes again, this time more fiercely. Just as my knees buckle, Tristan is there. Catching me. Like he always has. I'm hovering inches from his face, those impossibly deep blue eyes riveted on me.

<You can do this, Plant Girl. I know you can. We're close now.>

I'm well aware of how close we are—and I'm not talking about the distance to the lab. As he holds me, one arm around my waist and the other steadying my legs, I'd swear a slight flush colors his cheeks.

I feel heat rising in my own at the nearness of him, the feel of his breath on my cheek. Before my grip of the English language can be fully drowned out by my pounding heart, a man's deep voice interrupts us, drawing my attention away from Tristan. "Miss Johnson? Are you all right?"

I glance up to find that one of the agents has

paused beside me, staring at my odd posture, nearly on my knees in the dust. "I'm fine, thanks. Just lost my footing."

Tristan releases me, and I manage to stand on my own feet. Though I'm not sure I want to, rubbing my bare shoulders at the absence of his warmth.

The agent is still watching me closely, and I glance ahead to find that we've fallen behind the group. Brushing the dust off my jeans, I jog forward to catch up with the rest of the group. "What are these little earthquakes from, anyway?"

The agent's tone is unwavering. "Agent Maxoe thinks it's the effect of the rift merging our two worlds. This building can't take the fluctuations, which causes the tremors."

"Makes sense."

Keeping pace with the FBI, I edge closer to the side of the ramp, where I'll have a bit more privacy to carry on a one-sided conversation with my imaginary friend. I tilt my head toward the translucent young man who treads beside me.

Tristan absently rubs a hand against the back of his neck. <*Sorry about the earthquakes, Plant Girl.*

Maybe they'll get better the closer we get?>

"Will you ever stop calling me that silly nickname?" I tease softly, not intending to draw any more attention.

<I know it drives you crazy. But it's what I've called you since you were a kid. And as weird as it is, that nickname is something that's uniquely ours. And even when you tried to ignore me, you always reacted when I teased you with it.>

His shoulder nudges mine, sending a spiral of heat up my arm.

<I guess I'm just not ready to give up on any part of this.>

My throat is suddenly dry, but I manage to mumble, "And what is *this*?"

His mouth rises into a taunting smirk. *<I'm not sure yet.>*

"Well, let's hope we live long enough to find out."

Chapter Fourteen

As I continue to follow Agent Barstow down the ramp, his men surrounding me like a thick blanket of black suits, dark shadows seem to reach out with spindly fingers, grasping at my ankles. In spite of the body heat enveloping me, I shiver. The fraying hem of my crimson shirt is caked in dust. *I need a shower. Or better yet, a really long bath.*

Taking another step, I nearly plunge my foot off the edge of the ramp. With a gasp, I quickly step back into line behind Barstow, focusing on his rigid shoulders.

Barstow's clipped whispers catch my attention. I

can hardly make out his words, but his taut tone draws me closer.

"Say that again?"

He's speaking to Maxoe, who stands beside him, holding the Geiger counter. The younger agent's cheeks flush. "Sir, the numbers are continuing to climb. Whatever this breach is, it's giving off massive amounts of radioactive decay—and it seems to be growing."

"Define *massive*."

The dread in Maxoe's eyes must unnerve Barstow as much as it does me. The older agent holds up a hand, halting our movement. "Maxoe, what about the HAZMAT suits? Or anything to block the radioactivity?"

Maxoe shakes his head slowly, eyes glued to the Geiger counter again. "Sir, I'm afraid the numbers are climbing too fast. At this rate, we've already been contaminated. Besides, the HAZMAT suits wouldn't protect against radioactivity at this level, and we don't have time to have anything else flown in."

"We don't have time in general." Barstow mutters, running a hand through his bristled hair.

"We keep moving. In and out as quickly as possible. If we can't shut this thing down soon, this whole city is going to have a radioactive sunbath."

The agents clustered around me quickly agree, the tension rolling off their broad shoulders the only hint that they've been impacted by the news of the radioactive hotspot we're walking into.

Shaking off my own nervousness, I try to keep up as we shuffle forward at a faster pace. Voice low, I murmur to Tristan, "Let me know if you see anything out of the ordinary."

<You mean other than the ramp leading to a hidden lab? Or the shadows and vampires?>

I flash a wry look over my shoulder at him. "What are you even talking about? I thought you couldn't see anything on my side, anyway."

<Oh, I can see bits. Mostly what's around you. I'm just saying this place is seriously spooky.>

I squint at him. "How do you even know what a vampire is?"

His lips draw into a provocative smirk. *<You don't want to know.>*

Agent Maxoe, on my left, stumbles a bit. Trying

to cover up a chortle, he balances the Geiger counter in his hands. I can only imagine how strange this one-sided conversation must sound to him.

As we reach the bottom of the ramp, another tremor ripples through the ground.

The slope evens out into a long hallway with doors on both sides. More hallways lead from the main one. At least this area is better lit, with large overhead lights.

The room shakes again.

Barstow turns to Maxoe. "I need a status update."

Maxoe's brows knit together as his fingers speed over the device. "Wait, this can't be right."

Barstow shoulders his way through the other agents. "What's not right?"

"The device is malfunctioning. Must be too much information for it to compute. I'm afraid it could—"

His words are cut off by a long beep as the numbers on the screen start glitching, interrupted by a long dash and then a flash of white before it goes black. No amount of shaking from Barstow can convince it to turn back on.

Barstow swears. "What's going on, Agent?"

The man's hands shake. "The rift is continuing to expand but at a rate too fast for the Geiger counter to measure. It's tearing apart this area at a molecular level, and we don't have much time until it brings this entire building down on top of us."

The older agent groans, eyes darting around the dust-coated lab. He starts barking orders. "Split into pairs. Search every room. If you find anyone, get them out of the building as quickly you can. And if you discover any sign of the rift, call for backup."

Images of a little girl with red hair fill my thoughts. I start to run forward down the hallway toward the first door, but Barstow blocks my way. "You stay here. We can't have someone untrained getting underfoot. If I need a consultation, I'll call you."

While I fume in the hallway, placating him till I can slip out behind his back, the rest of the agents move out with the swift, deliberate actions of men who've trained their whole lives for moments like this. Knees bent, guns raised, they stalk around the corners of the hallway, each one targeting a different room.

"Clear!" The word comes from the stocky agent

nearest me and is repeated by the other teams.

I expect a confrontation every time a door is opened. But as each agent comes up empty, dread weighs down my heart. When I spent time here, every room was filled with either lab equipment or a patient held captive. Never had this underground facility been so deserted, with not even the doors locked.

What could make an entire lab of scientists and doctors flee without even bothering to turn out the lights? If they'd intended to evacuate before the FBI could find them, they did a terrible job of covering their tracks.

"Tristan!" I squint into the hazy sand dunes that blend with the lab around me. "Do you know where the Rhoon is?"

<I'm working on that!> His voice sounds distant.

I filter my gaze over the rusted structures that pierce through all sides of the facility. I see my friend scaling the top of a twisted metal tower.

A chorus of shouts snaps my attention back to the FBI scouring the laboratory. A few agents are attempting to drag two men in white lab coats out of a room. Scientists. Even their loping gait seems familiar.

While one leans heavily upon an agent, head slumped so that I can't make out his expression, the other man tries to wrestle his way out of their grasp.

When the scientist struggling against the agents sees me, his eyes widen. "You. This is all because of you!"

With a snarl, he breaks from the FBI agent's hold and bolts toward me, anger livid in his features. Before he can reach me, Tristan appears, knees bent in a stance that makes him look like a predator about to pounce.

He lurches toward the scientist, flicking his wrists to send his flails catapulting forward. One length of chain wraps around the man's legs, pulling them out from under him. The scientist plummets to his knees, but before he can scramble up again, the metal sphere at the end of Tristan's other flail nicks the edge of his head, dropping him like a rock. A thin stream of blood drips from his temple, but I see his chest moving, so I know he's still alive.

My jaw drops. *No wonder he could fend off the Rhoon for so many years.*

This time, however, he wasn't fighting off a

monster—at least not one made of leathery skin. He was protecting me, as he's always done.

My *thank you* feels so insufficient, but it still draws a grin from him.

Tristan wipes off the trickle of blood staining the weapons with the edge of his sleeve and stows them back in his leather pack.

The FBI agents drag the remaining scientist toward us. Unlike his counterparts, this man can hardly stand, let alone fight. When the scientist looks up, however, my muscles go limp. Frozen.

"Dr. Richards?" The lab coat is different, but the face definitely belongs to the man I've sat across from twice a week during therapy for the past six months. The psychiatrist who tried to convince me I was insane. "What are you doing here?"

"You know this man?" Barstow has arrived. His gaze darts between me and the man I once considered a confidant.

"He's my shrink."

"I doubt that," Barstow growls. "I knew it was strange when your records didn't have a Dr. Richards listed."

Someone down the hall calls for Barstow, his voice urgent.

"Surround her," Barstow orders his agents. "And get any information out of the doctor you can." Then he strides away.

Richards's face is pallid, and he's shaking. So am I. These scientists who stole me away and put a chip in my head have been following my every footstep.

And now they have Elinore.

"Where is my niece?" My fingers wrap around his neck before I know what I'm doing.

His bloodshot eyes loll toward me, and a stream of blood drips from the side of his mouth. My grip loosens. The broken human before me is a shell of the man I remember. Whatever did this to him, it was merciless.

The terror etched across his face slowly turns to recognition. "You. Your eyes..."

"What about my eyes?"

"We could never replicate the things you can see. None of the others survived the surgery." He coughs, releasing more blood. "When you escaped, we tried to follow. But something protected you. Becoming your therapist was my idea..."

His words trail off, eyes growing vacant. I push him into the grinding sand. "Tell me where Elinore is!" I half expect the agents who grip the doctor's arms to push me away, but they don't flinch. Neither does Richards, leaving my question unanswered.

"What's wrong with you? Tell me where she is!"

Tristan lays a hand on my shoulder. *<He has the disease that took my people.>*

I yank my hands away and step back. "Is it contagious?"

<No. The only way to get infected is by contact with the disease itself. The Rhoon in its airborne state. Even if that happened, I doubt it would affect you since you're straddling two worlds. Not in either world fully enough for the disease to take root. It can't infect someone who isn't physically there in the first place.>

The agents who have been standing a few feet away move closer, eyes roving the perimeter, then focusing on the scientist in front of me.

My attention is diverted when the sallow-skinned man lying on the floor tries to speak. "We were s-so desperate to f-find…we knew there was something else out there." A furious coughing fit stops his words. Blood fills his mouth, and he weakly attempts to spit it out. "We n-never expected it was…death incarnate."

The blood continues to bubble from his mouth, but this time it doesn't stop. The man that played a part in holding me captive as a lab experiment falls into the clutches of a death brought on by something so horrific it's broken even his mind. I almost feel bad for him.

The shrill cry of a child splits the air around us.

I bolt toward the room at the end of the hall. Barstow and several FBI agents cluster around the entrance. I shove past them. Just before my foot crosses the threshold, Agent Barstow steps in front of me, his broad shoulders immovable. Standing on my tiptoes, I peer over the sleeve of his jacket.

A silver operating table sits in the middle of the room with a small figure in a hospital gown restrained on it. Elinore's little wrists are chafed. Casts cover one arm and one leg. Her swollen eyelids are buttoned tightly as she wails in terror.

A small metal table is on its side, tools scattered

around it, along with vials of blood, medical files, and X-rays. Like it was knocked over in someone's desperation to flee the room—but they didn't have time to finish prepping Elinore for whatever procedure they were about to perform.

Instead, they left her alone. And frightened to death.

Fingernails clawing into Barstow's suit, I spit out, "Why aren't you helping her?"

He tilts his head, motioning to something behind Elinore.

A massive, splintering crack has formed in the white wall behind my niece, spreading out into a spiderweb of fractures. Everything those slivers touch turns iridescent—fluctuating between the underground facility and the apocalyptic backdrop on the opposite side of the rift. The charred bluish hue crackles and pops like it's living energy that absorbs anything it touches.

The rift. But why is it here of all places?

I glance around the room once more, and realization slowly fills in the dark corners and empty walls as I remember another surgery that took place here.

Mine.

When they implanted a chip in my head that tore this rift open in the first place. And now, with my newly strengthened connection to the rift—to Tristan—this window between worlds has opened wide enough to fracture an entire wall.

The fluctuating energy crackles again, and I can almost smell the scent of death leaking through from Tristan's world. *I did this…*

"You stay here," Barstow insists, his words interrupting my reverie. "I'm going to take three agents into the room and attempt to get the child out safely."

I step back, fingers twisting the red fabric of my tank top.

"Cover me," he barks. He inches carefully into the room, flanked on each side by agents. Two of them hold clear, rectangular shields with *FBI* engraved on them. As if that could hold back the Rhoon.

Barstow speaks softly to Elinore as they circle the table, stepping over the tools lying forgotten on the floor. Dust speckles the white room. I wipe at my bare arms, and a light dusting covers me as well.

Stretching to peer around the agent who's taken Barstow's place blocking me from the room, I raise my voice. "El, they're here to help you. Be brave, honey."

Her shrieks subside. The two agents holding shields cover Barstow's back as their superior starts to cut through Elinore's bonds with a blade. The remaining two agents stand on the other side of the table, working on the straps holding Elinore's legs. Their gazes constantly lurch back to the tear in the opposite wall.

The rift explodes. With an ear-splitting sucking sound, the cracks expand in an angry ripple of energy. A coppery mist leaks through the crevices and slithers toward the operating table. The thick haze separates into tendrils, wrapping around one of the agents guarding Barstow's back. It dissolves his writhing torso, swarms over his head, and swallows him whole.

Seconds later, the slick tendrils turn toward the other humans in the room. The mist spreads out, wafting toward their faces and setting the room in an uproar of hacking and coughing.

"Out!" Barstow bellows, and the agents rush toward the door. But it's too late. One man is gone before Barstow gives the order, and another claws across the floor as the disease devours him from the inside out.

Barstow makes it through the door, but nothing remains of three of the agents but a few bleached bones.

Chapter Fifteen

The mist changes direction, wrapping itself around the operating table Elinore is strapped to.

"No!" I rush forward. But a rough hand grabs my arm, dragging me back. Tristan's angry words are muted by the blood pounding in my ears, but when he pins me against the opposite wall, my breathing begins to slow.

<It won't kill Elinore. If that were its plan, it would have done so by now.>

I try to wrestle myself from his grip. "Then what is it doing?"

<That creature is a hunter. It's using Elinore as

bait. It'll devour anyone who tries to get close to her.
Including you.>

I blow out an exasperated breath, pounding my knuckles against the metal plating of his armor. I'm tired of getting pushed around by men who say they're trying to keep me safe. I don't want to be safe. I want to save my family. "There has to be some way to help her. To draw it away."

Barstow and the remaining agents stand a few feet from the entry to the operating room. Their pistols are aimed at the doorway, as if they can destroy the airborne killer with bullets. In spite of their rigid stances, they look pale. Barstow doubles over as a cough shakes his bulletproof vest.

"They're infected."

The agents' eyes all turn to me.

"We're fine," Barstow snaps, but he's clearly not even convincing himself.

Elinore is frozen on the table, her tiny chest hardly rising and falling as the sandy cloud surrounding her begins to recede toward the rift. When it draws away from her table, she sucks in a long gasp.

Elinore needs help. But if the agents try to enter

that room again, they'll die. On the other hand, they're already dying of the disease.

"Tristan, how much time do they have?"

<They only inhaled the disease and weren't engulfed by it like those other men. That means they have a fighting chance—but only if they get out of here now. The more they come in contact with the sand— the contaminant—the worse it will get. You saw my world. It's covered in sand, and it's a desolate wasteland.>

I straighten, meeting Barstow's gaze full on. "Get your men out of here. If you stay here, in contact with the dust, the disease will only get worse."

Beads of sweat form on his forehead. "And what are you going to do?"

"I'm not sure. But I think I'm immune to the disease. And I have Tristan. We'll figure something out."

His jaw tightens, and a war of duty and survival plays behind his gray eyes.

Finally he jerks his chin in a half-hearted nod. Raising a shaky finger, he taps his earpiece. "Laurinski, send for HAZMAT suits. We're pulling out." He looks back at me. "I suppose even if I ordered you to come back with us, you wouldn't."

"Sorry, sir."

His quivering hand drops onto my shoulder. Then he pulls a thin knife with a black grip from his nylon belt and places it in my hands. "Good luck."

As he directs his remaining men toward the ramp, I pray the disease in their bodies doesn't worsen. When the click-clack of their footsteps fades to silence, I'm left in an abandoned underground lab with a young man only I can see.

Just like old times.

Gripping the knife, I turn to Tristan and find him deep in thought, his attention riveted on the ceiling. *<Once the Rhoon realizes you're immune, it will attack you. I'll try to distract it while you get Elinore out of there.>*

"You can do that?"

<Once you get Elinore to safety, we'll figure out how to trap it here and stop that thing for good.>

My vision blurs as I envelop Tristan in a hug.

<I won't be able to hold that monster off for long. So as soon as Elinore is safe, meet me at the rift.>

I pull back and study his face, the way his eyes darken when he's worried. I'm going to miss this friend of mine if we can't stop the Rhoon.

"I'll get back to you as soon as I can," I say. "Then we'll kick this thing's tail."

That draws a slight smile from his chapped lips. All too soon, he turns away and races through the underground facility. Only, to him, it isn't a lab. It's a decaying canyon with a steep cliff on one side, rimmed by a dark haze that's filtering into my world.

Elinore's terrified screams snap my attention back to her. "El, take deep breaths! I'm going to save you." *Somehow.* "Hang on!"

Her screams turn to hiccupping sobs.

Some of the mist still lingers around Elinore, so I force myself to wait outside the room until it has all slunk back into Tristan's world. Holding my breath, I watch the mist filter through the rift, praying it doesn't decide to change tactics and use Elinore as prey instead of bait.

It only appears to have one target, however—the blond young man drawing it away from the edge of the lab. My eyes trace the dust as it disperses from the room Elinore's in to the opposite side of the rift, spilling into the sand dunes that cover the landscape. Once he's put a good amount of distance between the mist and us, Tristan turns with determination toward the creature, his flails dangling from his hands. Their sharp ends drag in the musty sand, creating dual trails behind him.

My hold tightens on my knife as the haze rises to meet him, encircling but unable to sway the lanky young warrior. Then the mist begins to congeal into a solid form—cavernous, powerful. Towering over Tristan like a mountain.

It takes the shape of a humanlike creature with a thick hide, the same tarnished color as the sand. Arms so solid they could easily topple a building, with claws for hands. Slivers of rock that jut from its forepaws. Its head has no features except for a gaping jaw that looks ready to suck in anything nearby.

I start forward as it reaches for Tristan, but his voice explodes in my mind. *<Save Elinore!>*

I streak into the operating room, careful to avoid the cracked pylons and rusted remnants of Tristan's world jutting through the walls of the lab as I reach

Elinore's side. "Hey, baby. I'm here now. I'm going to get you out. And Tristan is going to help us."

Her big eyes focus on me. "Tristan is here?"

"Yes. After I get you out, we'll see him together. You'd like that, right?"

Her bottom lip quivers, but she nods.

"Good. Now, we have to be really quiet. Can you do that for me?"

Her whimpers go silent.

Watching the rift out of the corner of my eye, I saw away at the leather restraints with Barstow's blade. The Rhoon could burst back through that crevice at any moment.

I finish slicing through the material holding Elinore's arms. Leaning over her, I smooth back the damp curls plastered to her forehead and quickly pat her shoulder under the oversized hospital gown she's wearing. "Almost there…"

I resume my work on the restraints holding her legs. My heart leaps as the last sheath of leather snaps. She tumbles into my arms.

After wrapping her tightly against my chest, careful of the casts on her arm and leg, I drop the knife and bolt out of the room. Fighting back tears of relief, I race down the hallway.

Dust shifts beneath my feet. The tile floor dissolves into sand. The end of the facility morphs into a desolate wasteland. We're surrounded by broken cities and dark skies and a sun that glows several shades too red.

My feet stop moving when I catch sight of Tristan. He is perched on the roof of a sloping construction that must have once been a tower. He's almost level with the top of the looming Rhoon.

I feel the hot wind of the dead world on my cheeks, drafting through the rips in my red tank top.

The rift is opening farther, blurring all lines between the two worlds. I can't tell if it's doing so of its volition or mine—probably both.

"Do you see that?" I whisper to my niece.

Through fingers fanned over her eyes, she nods. "It's Tristan!"

A good half mile away from us, he stands on the edge of the sloping tower, flails spinning in dual circles on both sides of his body as he dances around the hulking creature. He taunts it, moving close enough to draw its attention, then leaping back out of reach. He sends the barbed weight at the end of his handle flying toward the Rhoon. The metal slams into the pallid, leathery flesh of the creature.

The Rhoon swipes at Tristan with an immense, clawed paw. He barely evades its grasp. The game of keep-away continues. But he can't stay out of its reach forever.

"El, I need to help Tristan, so I'm going to try to get you out of here now. Okay?"

Her arms tighten around my neck, the scratchy material of her hospital gown against my skin, and I sprint to the bottom of the ramp. Leaving the lab behind, I scale the upward slope, my shins burning as I force my legs to churn faster. I burst through the top of the ramp into the fake blood bank and almost collide with Agent Barstow.

He stands at the top of the incline, dressed in a bulky yellow HAZMAT suit. "I'll take her and find a nurse. The rest of my men are recovering." His voice sounds strange through the thin plastic covering his mouth.

"How did you know I'd be here?"

He scoops Elinore from my arms. "I had a hunch you might need someone on this side."

"Thank you." I could almost hug him.

Nestled in the agent's arms, Elinore reaches the hand not covered in a cast toward me. I kiss her forehead and promise to be back as soon as I can.

Now that she's safe, I can help Tristan.

I head back down the ramp toward the rift. Toward the imaginary friend who is so much more than that.

My shoes kick up a cloud of dust as I trudge forward, the ramp disappearing beneath the sandy floor. Squinting through the thick, golden-orange fog that spreads around me, I break into a run, shouting Tristan's name.

The mist crawls into my nose and down my throat. When I try to cough it up, the darkening fumes sting my eyes. My hair is thick with it, the shoulder-length tangles sticking to my face. Wrenching a hairband off my wrist, I tie it back. This is the airborne disease that destroyed an entire planet. I only hope we manage to find the rift in time.

"Tristan! Where are you?"

<Over here!> His words are accentuated by a moan.

I bat the mist out of my face to make out his silhouette in the distance.

The Rhoon nearly blends into the swirling mist, but I can see its intimidating form standing in front of Tristan. My friend has lowered into a crouch, flails hanging motionless. The Rhoon lumbers forward. When it's inches away, Tristan springs up. He races toward the monster, and his flails whip around his head, slamming into the beast's rock-hard flesh with such force it tears chunks away. The Rhoon snarls and bats at him again, its fist catching the side of Tristan's body and crumpling him to the ground.

He is back on his feet quickly, leaping around the next swipe and pushing the towering beast back a pace. He tries to dodge the Rhoon again, but it blocks him with surprising speed for its bulk. A wash of red spray splatters through the dark haze, sending chills down my spine.

I gag on the fog. The dust presses in on me like gravity. I struggle to stay upright. My skin is burning hot, like it's been scorched by acid. In spite of how much of it must have gathered to solidify into that creature, there seems to be no end to the sand. I can barely make out the shapes around me.

But I have to keep moving forward. I need to find the rift.

The mist is a thousand tiny pinpricks of tarnished gold, swirling around me and hiding nearly everything from view.

My body aching, I sink to my knees and find that I can see better low to the ground. I search through the fog for anything unnatural that might represent a tear in the fabric of space and time.

Then I see it. Ahead of me, whirling above the sand-coated ground, is a six-foot-tall rippling window. Mist pours through a gap in the surface, turning into a thin, wafting substance that crackles like lightning the minute it leaks through.

And on the other side, with its back to me, is the menacing form of the Rhoon. Almost like it's standing guard. Placing itself directly between Tristan and the rift.

"Tristan! The rift is behind that creature!"

His head tips toward me for an instant. Then he's

jerked back into the battle, flails spinning wildly as he attempts to stay out of the Rhoon's reach.

Every time he dodges away, the Rhoon corners him again. It pins him against a crumbling house and slams a massive fist into his side. No matter how many times he finds the strength to rise, the creature pounds him into the sand again.

Tristan's side drips crimson, the stitches tearing as he desperately tries to escape the Rhoon.

He's not going to make it. If I don't do something soon, he'll pass out—or worse.

I search for something to use as a weapon.

Who am I kidding? I'm no warrior. I couldn't stop that thing.

The Rhoon knocks him down again. Tristan's body convulses as he struggles to drag himself to his feet. He won't survive the next attack.

Do something!

"Hey!"

The word is out of my mouth before I realize it. The Rhoon's mountainous form, bent over Tristan and poised for the kill, freezes. Turns. Looks right at me.

My first instinct is to do what I always do—hide.

Stay quiet, try to melt away and not draw attention. Survive.

But I don't want to just survive. I want to live. For Elinore.

And Tristan.

Throwing my shoulders back, I wave a hand at the Rhoon. "You want me? I'm here. In your world. Have at it."

Chapter Sixteen

The Rhoon turns fully, snarls at me, and then disappears in a gust of sand. Tristan stumbles backward from the blast, chest heaving as he tries to catch his breath. Even from this distance, I see confusion in his eyes.

The dunes of glimmering dust pooling around me start to gather, growing into the towering form of the Rhoon inches from my feet. The creature materializes into its solid form like a great rhinoceros rising from its sleep. Thick limbs. Jagged claws.

And I'm defenseless.

Taking a few steps backward, I peer around the

creature to see Tristan dragging his aching body toward the rift. He won't reach it for several minutes. By that time, it'll be too late.

At least someone will remember me.

Tipping up my chin, I face the monster as it lumbers forward, swinging arms like pillars of rock. An unusual calm sweeps over me.

Today I am not the girl whose parents didn't love her. Or the woman who's crazy. Or the aunt who can't keep a job.

I am the girl who can see what no one else can.

I matter. At least this once.

The Rhoon raises a clawed paw. I manage to dodge its first swipe, but the second one is too quick. The curving talons slice through my chest, tearing my shirt.

And pass right through my skin. Like I don't exist in his world.

Fact is, I don't.

An abrupt pain hits me as the monster's arm sweeps through my body, but it leaves no physical damage. *I'm alive?*

Laughter bubbles up, unexpected and wild,

driving the Rhoon into frenzy. I take a step closer. "I guess you picked on the wrong girl."

I'm the girl who tore a hole in the fabric of space and time. Who caused two parallel worlds to collide. And yet, while I somehow have one foot on each side, I'm not completely a part of either.

Just as I walked through the walls of the hospital, so the Rhoon's continued attempts at striking my body pass through me. Again and again, its lumbering swipes have no effect.

Finally, it opens its cavernous jaw and releases a hair-raising shriek—then dissolves. The wind kicks up dust that swirls around me in mini tornadoes. Pulling at my torn clothes, pelting my exposed skin, stinging my eyes behind closed lids. Clouding my vision so that I can no longer see where the rift is.

Dropping to my knees, I crawl forward. The sand cuts at my skin, burning my legs. I can't draw in a decent breath. While the Rhoon couldn't touch me, this fury of sand is making a wonderful attempt at suffocating me.

Fingers clawing into the dust, I wrench forward, trying to keep a clear head when the world is anything but clear. The shimmer of the rift looms only a few feet ahead, but my body hardly responds to my mental commands anymore. I drag my limp frame a few feet more before it gives out completely and I collapse into the dust.

Only yesterday I was worrying about losing my job. Now I'm trying to escape an airborne disease secreted by a creature from another world. What a way to die.

No. I just survived that creature head-on. I am not going out like this.

A growl starts in the back of my throat as I drag myself to my knees.

But they refuse to hold me up a second longer. My legs give out, heavy and bleeding, just like the rest of my body.

When I was a child, I would have waited for my hero to come rescue me. But this time he can't help.

Maybe that's the point. Tristan saved me so that I could be strong enough to save myself, if only this once. I'm no longer the scared little girl hiding behind an operating table. He has shown me how to turn my weaknesses into strengths.

Swiping the dust away from my face, I force my weary bones to push me to my feet. Air floods my lungs, and the blackness starts to flicker away from my vision. I suck in more oxygen, spitting out the sand that comes with it. I force one foot after the other.

The vivid electricity of the rift cuts through the dust just a few feet away. Beyond it, Tristan's gaze settles on me. The Rhoon is nowhere to be seen.

My eyes latch onto Tristan as I stumble close enough for him to catch my shoulders. Blood soaks through his blue armor, like the first time he saved me as a child. My hero. The one who told me I could do anything and that no one else's opinion mattered. The one who always saw *me*.

<*And you said you weren't a warrior.*> Pride beams from his tired smile.

I wrap my bleeding hands around his and let him pull me to safety. As we limp closer to the rift, the whirling dust storm abates.

"So, how do we end this?" My voice is hoarse.

He releases my hands and steps around to stand on the opposite side of the rift. His image wavers like water behind the deep tear. In the distance, the Rhoon is beginning to re-solidify.

<We have to reach through and touch each other. Fully connect, so that the tear between the two parallel worlds can be stabilized.>

I stare at him. We've already touched several times. How is this different? Because we're reaching through the rift? There's something about this I don't understand. It makes me feel uneasy.

<Ready?>

Not hardly. But I nod anyway. I'll ask him for clarification when we're safely through this.

I extend my right arm, letting my fingertips brush the edge of the rift, then push my hand all the way through. The energy swirls around my arm, sending jolts through my veins. It doesn't hurt, but the suction is the strongest force I've ever felt.

I flex my fingers, waiting for something to happen. Just when I'm about to pull back, a strong hand grabs hold of mine. The suction that has been threatening to tear my arm off ceases.

I feel Tristan in a way that's more physical than any of the glimpses I've been allowed before. I'm not just reaching into his world—I'm actually a part of it.

Beneath my touch, I can feel every rough scar on his palm and the thin lines of his skin.

<Focus on me, on this link we have. Solidify the connection.>

Gripping his palm tighter, I do as he instructs. Since this bond has become second nature, it takes only seconds for the rest of the landscape to fade away. The rift's whirling electricity subsides to a low hum, and the shifting material calms into a glass-like state. I can see him clearly now, on the other side of this window between worlds.

His mouth smiles, but his eyes hold deep pain. The wound to his side must be aching terribly after fighting that creature.

"The rift is stable. Now you have to come through. Then we'll close it completely. After that, we'll get you some medical attention."

His darkening expression makes me bite my lip as a sickening doubt slithers in my mind.

<Now that we've solidified the connection, we have to cut it off completely.>

"What? Are you crazy?"

<Fern, we can't shut the rift unless we're on

opposite sides. I have to stay here. Besides, I can't
come through if we're still connected. I'm tied to this
world the way you're linked to the rift.>

"I don't understand."

<Our connection started the rift. And I'm *why*
you've never been able to close it. I represent this
world, and I'm your link to it.>

"I can't give up this connection. I can't give *you*
up."

<You have to. It's the only way. If you cut me off
completely, you'll close the rift and save your world.>

Tears make dirty streaks down my cheeks. "I
can't lose you. You're the only real friend I have." I
wipe at the tears with my free hand. "You're more
than that. Please don't ask me to do this."

Just as he opens his mouth, he's thrown violently
to the side. His grip on me almost slips, but my other
hand dives in, grabbing onto his fingers.

"Tristan!"

A hulking shadow materializes behind him. The
Rhoon has hardened again, cracked and lumbering.
Tristan struggles to his feet, dodging to the side as the
Rhoon swipes at him. Somehow, he still clings to my

hands.

<Plant Girl, you have to end this now.>

The stupid nickname makes the tears fall faster. My body shakes as I watch him slowly rise to his feet, dragging himself closer to the rift while keeping one eye on the Rhoon.

If I try to let go and help him, we'll lose the connection. But if I close the rift and leave him there, he won't make it.

His gaze clings to my face for a few precious seconds. *<This is the only way to save your world.>*

A sledgehammer barrels into my chest. "Why would you give up your life for a world that doesn't even believe you exist?"

A cough wracks his body, but his grip on me remains strong. *<Because I believe everyone should have the chance to live.>*

A massive claw digs into Tristan's back, but he still doesn't let go of my hand.

My knees buckle, but before my jeans hit the floor, Tristan pulls me up again. *<You know, this isn't how I thought things would go. I wanted to spend the rest of my life catching you when you fall.>* His voice is too soft. Too breathless.

Pouring strength into my hollow limbs, I tighten my hold on his shaking palm. "You already have."

My hands grip his armor, pulling him closer. His wide blue eyes, now completely devoid of pain and sparking with intensity, are the last thing I see before my mouth crashes against his. I kiss him, letting my touch say everything that's been building up in me. Let my actions speak the volumes my words don't have time to.

I need him to know that he's the best thing that's ever happened to me.

Tristan groans softly. He leans in closer through the rift, hands cupping my face, deepening the kiss in a way that makes my head spin. Both of the worlds swirling around me fade away until all I'm aware of is him. His plans—the things he'd secretly wished for. I feel as though I can see the innermost places of his thoughts.

I see myself in his mind, wearing a lacy white dress and veil. Behind us is a small house that's very much *ours*. Where Elinore is a cousin, holding a sleeping baby girl with Tristan's golden-blond hair and my splash of freckles.

He wanted to protect me until there was nothing left but the two of us. He'd intended to be my hero for the rest of our lives.

I wish I could spend my life trying to be deserving of this man. For so long, all I'd wanted was for him to be gone. Now I'd rather stay in this dying land forever. With him.

But that's impossible.

Like a dying summer breeze, the images dissolve. Desperately wanting to pull them back, I cling harder to him, drinking in every aspect of this moment that I can.

I finally sink back down, still feeling the heat of his touch. "I would never wish you away, not for the world."

But I cannot keep using him. I can't hold him here simply because I want him. My whole life our relationship has depended on my whims, my needs.

No longer. This time I have to love him enough to do the hardest thing. Let him go.

His squeeze on my hands is so light, it's as if he's given me every reserve of strength he had. I almost break down right there. Instead, I grit my teeth and do something that will never leave my nightmares.

I let go.

Tears leak through my lashes when I feel his hand dissolve from my grasp.

Pushing Tristan away, I shut down a core part of me that has always believed he was real. All the moments he's saved me. All the brushes with his world.

I close the rift.

Its energy flares one last time, enveloping my body in blue light. Then it vanishes.

A cool breeze rustles my hair. I slowly open my eyes. I'm standing on a patch of crumbled cement, a starry night sky overhead, California skyscrapers igniting the skyline.

The only thing in front of me is a lone white wall of the underground lab, where the rift had once fractured a deep schism.

I'm on a plateau of smoldering ashes and charred metal. What had once been an underground facility, and above that, a children's hospital, is now reduced to scrap metal in the wake of the rift's closing. With the memories those places provoke, I can't bring myself to feel guilty that they've been demolished.

I wrap my arms around my bare shoulders, suddenly freezing cold.

Dozens of FBI agents run toward me, their dark-suited forms intermingled with a red-and-white sea of firemen and medics. They crowd around me, asking questions all at once and flashing lights in my face.

Agent Barstow steps closer, raising a hand to still the barrage of questions, then asks his own. "Are you all right? What happened?"

"We closed the rift." The words sound like they're coming from someone else.

Too numb to answer any of his other questions, I stumble toward my niece, who's wrapped in a blanket. A nurse is checking her casts and applying salve to her swollen face.

I sink to the dusty gravel, nearly too tired to put my arms around Elinore when she drags herself into my lap. A few people hesitantly pat my back and offer congratulations my mind cannot process.

The entire world says we won, but all I feel is loss. Terrible loss.

Chapter Seventeen

Three Months Later

"And I'll have two Big Belly Burgers with fries and a Dr Pepper."

My fingers work quickly, scribbling down the order on the pad in my hand. "Is that all?"

The family of four nods. I stash the pen and paper in one of the large pockets of my waitressing uniform, but I can't move. I just stare at them. They look so content. Safe. They have no idea that they owe their lives to a young man only I knew existed. If I tried to tell them who he was and what he'd done, they'd call me crazy.

I'm probably the sanest person here.

Shaking my head, I start back across the restaurant. The floor seems so clean—no rusted buildings piercing through to scare me half to death. Part of me expects a certain mischievous voice to whisper in my ear or brush a hand against my shoulder. Instead, my journey back through the diner is dull and uneventful.

My muscles still ache, and scars cover my legs and arms, but nothing else remains as a testament to what I lost to save this world. Nothing remains of *him*.

Yet, with every breath, I swear to never forget—to never stop seeing the world as he did. And maybe I'll show others how to do that as well.

Time passes slowly. But when my shift finally ends, I nearly run out the front door.

"Mind if I sit here?" I ask a woman on the bus, pointing to the empty window seat beside her.

She mutters, "Yes," without even looking up.

Clutching my purse to my chest, I slide past her into the seat.

As the bus starts moving, beginning its route toward Los Angeles, the overhead television turns on, displaying recent news. An all-too-familiar image flashes on the screen, and a reporter announces, "The dramatic story of the St. Matthew's Children's Hospital fire continues, three months after the disaster."

The ashen remains of the hospital, still jarring with its ragged boulders and twisted spikes of metal, are vividly displayed. Then the screen flashes to an empty hospital bed.

"A man who was seriously wounded in the incident was recently released from the Jefferson-Davies Medical Center."

I turn away, the images nothing more than a reminder of pain. Of people who survived and moved on with their lives. Of those who didn't. And a deep ache at Tristan's absence.

As the reporter's voice fills the background, I dig out a pad of paper from my knapsack. I flip it open, balancing it on one knee, and shuffle the pages. I stop at a white sheet decorated with a freehand sketch of a young man with stark blue eyes and hair cut jagged just above his slim shoulders. And a smirk that is simultaneously teasing and reassuring.

Taking out my pencil, I retrace the lines on his jaw, highlighting the scars there. With every stroke of the pencil, the broken pieces in my chest throb a little less. At least this way, I can still see him.

"That's really good!"

I'm surprised to find the woman sitting beside me leaning over to look at the sketch. "He's cute. Your boyfriend?"

I tighten my hold on the paper, lead smudging the pad of my thumb. "No. He is a…best friend."

Was. Was a best friend.

"He certainly has personality."

"You have no idea."

I turn toward the empty seat across the aisle, letting my thoughts wander dangerously, envisioning the imaginary friend who once sat there. Blinking back the tears that blur my view, I turn to look out the window. The sky is so broad, so vivid. Endless. Almost like a world all its own.

For most of my life, I was desperate to feel like I belonged here. In this city, on this planet. Now my eyes are always drawn to the sky.

My chest aches for a world few even knew

existed.

Chapter Eighteen

When Elinore and I make it back to the apartment after I pick her up from daycare, she's beyond excited to show me her new craft project. As she prepares to unveil her creations across our kitchen table, my phone buzzes.

A text informs me that the number for Dr. Richards is no longer in service, and his disappearance is being looked into.

"El, give me a second."

I duck into our room. Leaning against the closed door, I find his contact info on my phone. As my finger hovers over the delete button, I stare at the last link to a world that dissolved when the FBI released a testimony verifying my sanity—almost as if the nightmare of being insane had never existed.

It didn't.

Seeing Tristan had never been the nightmare. My desire to be "normal" was—to become something I was never meant to be. Safe and complacent. To survive but not to live.

"There's so much more than that."

I tap the button and watch as Dr. Richards's contact info is erased with a *ding.*

"Good-bye, Doctor."

When I make my way back out to the kitchen, Elinore's brows rise. "What are you so happy about?"

"Oh, nothing. Now, where's this masterpiece of yours?"

I sink into a kitchen chair, and she shuffles into my lap. After opening her pink backpack, she carefully lifts out her creation. It's a doll made out of modeling clay, about the size of my hand. It wears a green dress and has stringy red hair.

"Do you know who this is?" She peers up at me expectantly.

I nuzzle her close. "Hmm...is it your sister,

Rosetta?" Her little nose wrinkles, and I laugh. "I'll take that as a *no*. Is it Grandma Stone?"

She playfully punches my arm. "Stop it! It's you, Aunt Fern."

"Really?" I hold the doll reverently. "She's lovely, El. Thank you."

She squirms in my lap, digging into her backpack again. "I have one more."

She lifts a second clay figure, this one wearing a red shirt and blue pants, with curls of unruly yellow hair. My mouth goes dry.

Elinore lifts him up, her mouth pinched to the side. "It's your friend. The one you drew as a little girl. The one who saved us."

I gently take the doll, holding the soft clay carefully. So many emotions race through my head.

Elinore's little hand covers mine. "I thought you could put him by your bed. That way, when you feel sad at night, you can look at him and don't have to cry."

My words catch in my throat, and I excuse myself, muttering something about dinner. The evening drags on, and after tucking Elinore into bed, I flop onto my mattress, exhausted.

But not exhausted enough to sleep.

Around four a.m., I push myself up onto my elbow and watch Elinore nestled beside me, the back of her fuzzy pajamas rising and falling as she sleeps. Shifting into a sitting position, I brush a hand over the bedside table, looking for my phone. Instead I bump into two small clay figures.

Lifting the tiny dolls into my lap, I stare at them. At him.

"Why can't I move on?" The whisper hangs in the air even as I slip from the bed and head into the kitchen to make myself some tea.

I sift through my tea bags but finally set the basket down. I rest my elbows on the counter, settling my head in my hands.

"Tristan, why can't I get you out of my head?"

I reach for a peppermint tea bag, my hands shaking as I fill a teapot with tap water. As I set it on the stove, something warm brushes against my shoulder. A hand gently tucks a strand of hair behind my ear.

I freeze, unable to breathe.

That's not Elinore…

Ever so slowly, I turn around. A shadowed form stands several inches taller than me, wearing jeans and a hoodie. As he leans down, the faint light from the rising sun ignites his mischievous blue eyes and the silver scars on his jaw. His lips part in a smile that sends shivers down my spine.

"Miss me, Plant Girl?"

His voice breaks the silence, this time loud and clear—no longer in my head.

I stand rooted to the spot, unable to believe my eyes. Unable to breathe. After three months, I'd given up hope of ever seeing that smile again.

His face has a healthy glow to it. He moves gingerly, which tells me his wounds are still mending. But his eyes are brilliant, vivid blue. Not a shadow to be seen. I've never seen him so…whole.

He scrubs a hand through his shoulder-length hair, loose curls dusting his forehead. "The jeans are a new look for me. Do you—"

I launch at him with a shriek. My body collides with his, arms around his neck, gripping him tightly. So tightly. With my cheek pressed against the fabric of his navy blue hoodie, I feel his heartbeat against my ear. His warmth spreads through my body. I tuck closer, desperate for proof that he's real.

"How...?"

His arms curl around me, and a soft laugh rumbles in his chest. "Remember how I said that our connection is what tied me to my world? Well, when you severed it, I was no longer directly tied to my world or to the rift."

He pauses, and the words slowly take root. When I'd been selfless enough to no longer use him, when I loved him enough to let him go, only then could he ever be mine in the first place. When my bond no longer held him to his world, I set him free. In giving Tristan up, I actually saved him.

He continues to talk, the sound like a salving balm to my ears.

"Just as the rift closed, I dove through. Somehow I made it. But with the time and space difference, I didn't land in your world for a few days. Then I was so banged up from my fight with the Rhoon, I passed out. I woke up in a hospital. Was in and out of consciousness for months as they patched me up.

About two weeks ago I was finally well enough to remember what I was doing here. Why Fern—" His rambling stops abruptly. "Are you crying?"

Tears roll down my cheeks, and I don't try to stop them.

His hands unwind from my waist, leaving me feeling cold—until they cup my face. His thumb brushes away the salty droplets as I blink up at his uncertain expression. Then my lips tilt in a gentle smile, and his eyes widen. As his smirk joins mine, an understanding flashes between us that causes my cheeks to flush.

With a sigh, he leans in, forehead resting against mine. It feels so natural. As if there had never been a world separating us.

"I'm here, Plant Girl," he whispers.

The words are as vivid and as hopeful and as *real* as he is.

Acknowledgements

Where to even start? I have been so tremendously blessed in this entire journey of putting my soul-story to paper.

My family—you have always been there to encourage me, to constantly point me to Christ, to remind me why I do this. To have the hard conversations and the late nights. I am so thankful that God gave me each of you.

Joanne Bischof—for late nights and spontaneous park play-dates to teach me formatting, craft, and everything in between. Your beautiful, strong heart shines through everything you do, and you never cease to inspire me.

Kezia Manchester—for always believing in me and these strangely beautiful stories—even when I didn't. You are a bright light, kindred spirit. (Also, for being Jude and never minding.)

Alysia M. and Emily H.—my adelphe sisters and critique-tribe extraordinaire. For simply being your sweet, talented selves.

Mick Silva—for believing in a nervous teen at a writers' conference. For pushing me past my limits, but never letting me doubt that the story He has put on my heart is worth penning. Your wisdom and talent have impacted this novella—and this author—in lasting ways.

Meghan Gorecki—the Peggy Carter to my Captain America. Always there when I need you, stronger than I can imagine, and able to rock that red lipstick. Thank you for the gentle ways you polished this novella into something wonderful. May we continue to trade stories and dreams.

Karen Magro—who would have known the ways God was preparing us to be friends and critique partners? Through something as painful as Lyme disease, He knew I'd need you at just the right time. Thank you for putting your everything into these stories and this girl. Your friendship means so much!

Charis Smith—it's always amazing to me to look back and see how far we've come. I would never have gotten serious about writing if it weren't for you and our little fantasy story, and for that I will be eternally grateful! My prayers and joy go with you as you start into this new phase of life. <3

Jenny—for giving Fern and Tristan's story the most beautiful face—ahem cover—ever. <3

Jaime at Rockstar *and Sandra at* Celebrate Lit—the cover reveal and release day tours were fantastic. Thank you for all the hard work and care you've put into them. You are stars!

My amazing Launch Team—you all are the lifeblood of this whole publishing journey, and make my life as an author such a joy. Thank you for being the stars that point me onward—you rock!

And to the countless others who have taught me so much along this journey. Who have poured themselves into me, into my stories, into my wounds and my words and my dreams. To the authors—and there are so many!—that I want to be just like. To all the talented people at *Go Teen Writers*. To my fellow Indie Authors—paving your own roads.

To the Author of my heart, these stories and this girl have always been Yours. Thank you for showing me that with you, Jesus, all things are possible.

Audiobook

Hear *The Girl Who Could See* brought to life on audio!

Available through Amazon & Audible

Also By Kara Swanson

Pearl of Merlydia

By Charis Smith and Kara Swanson

"Full of surprises and turns…reminiscent of C.S. Lewis."

About the Author

As the daughter of missionaries, *Kara Swanson* spent sixteen years of her young life in the jungles of Papua New Guinea. Able to relate with characters dropped suddenly into a unique new world, she quickly fell in love with the speculative genre. At seventeen, she released a fantasy novel, *Pearl of Merlydia*. Her short story is included in Kathy Ide's *21 Days of Joy: Stories that Celebrate Mom*. She has published many articles, including one in *Encounter* magazine, and she received the *Mount Hermon Most Promising Teen Writer* award in 2015.

Contact Me!

Find Kara online at karaswanson.com

Facebook: Kara Swanson, Author

Twitter: @kara_author

Instagram: @karaswanson_author